PENGUIN BOOKS

THE MAN WITH NO ENDORPHINS

James Gorman has written a monthly column entitled "Light Elements" for *Discover* magazine. His pieces have also appeared in *The New Yorker*, *The Atlantic*, and other magazines. He lives with his wife and two daughters outside New York City.

The MAN *with* NO ENDORPHINS

and other reflections on science by

JAMES GORMAN

PENGUIN BOOKS

PENGUIN BOOKS
Published by the Penguin Group
Viking Penguin Inc., 40 West 23rd Street,
New York, New York 10010, U.S.A.
Penguin Books Ltd, 27 Wrights Lane,
London W8 5TZ, England
Penguin Books Australia Ltd, Ringwood,
Victoria, Australia
Penguin Books Canada Ltd, 2801 John Street,
Markham, Ontario, Canada L3R 1B4
Penguin Books (N.Z.) Ltd, 182–190 Wairau Road,
Auckland 10, New Zealand

Penguin Books Ltd, Registered Offices:
Harmondsworth, Middlesex, England

First published in the United States of America by
Viking Penguin Inc. 1988
Published in Penguin Books 1989

10 9 8 7 6 5 4 3 2 1

All the essays in this book first appeared, some under different titles,
in *Discover* magazine.

Grateful acknowledgment is made for permission to use the following
copyrighted works:
    Excerpt from "Flushed From the Bathroom of Your Heart" by Jack
Clement. © 1967 by Jack Music, Inc.
    Excerpt from "You Don't Mess Around with Jim" by Jim Croce. © 1971,
1972 DenJac Music Co. & MCA Music Inc. All worldwide rights administered
by DenJac Music Co. Used by permission. All rights reserved.
    Excerpt from "Drinkin' Wine Spo-Dee-o-Dee, Drinkin' Wine" by Granville
"Stick" McGhee and Mayo Williams. © Copyright 1949, 1973 by MCA Music
Publishing, a division of MCA Inc., New York, NY 10019. Copyright renewed.
Used by permission. All rights reserved.
    Illustrations by Joe Le Monnier from *Discover* magazine, May 1986.
© *Discover* magazine 1986.

LIBRARY OF CONGRESS CATALOGING IN PUBLICATION DATA
Gorman, James, 1949–
The man with no endorphins.
1. Science—Anecdotes.   I. Title.
[Q167.G67 1989] 500   88–28965
ISBN 0 14 01.0359 7 (pbk.)

Printed in the United States of America
Set in Century Schoolbook

For my wife

Contents

Introduction

A number of years ago I wrote a short news item about something called a bezoar stone. At the time I was a serious science writer, which is to say that I wrote articles about serious science and I was serious while I wrote them. I had tackled some big subjects—stars, galaxies, black holes. But I was beginning to tire. I was beginning to feel that if you'd written one article about spiral galaxies, you'd written them all. Consequently, bezoar stones caught my attention.

They're remarkable objects. To quote myself in *The Sciences* (May/June 1979), "Bezoar stones are not actually stones at all, but concretions of partly digested and calcified hair that bump and jog for years along the alimentary canals of antelopes, goats and other ruminants." In other words—hair balls. They were renowned, somewhat renowned anyway, because legend had it that they offered protection against poisoning. Potentates of one sort or another used to dip these stones into glasses of wine they suspected might have been tampered with. Then they had somebody else drink the wine.

I wrote a news story about the stones because scientists had discovered that bezoar stones really worked, at least for one poison. They really did detoxify arsenic, somehow absorbing or trapping toxic molecules. The secret ingredients were partly digested hair and a mineral called brushite. All of which made for a pretty good story with a bit too much of this kind of talk: "The disulfide linkages in the stone's calcified hair protein are broken down, exposing sites for binding between sulfur and arsenite." (You can see why I gave up straight science writing.) However, what was most interesting to me about bezoar stones never got into the article. How, I wondered, did anybody get the idea to use bezoar stones in the first place?

To a man faced, day in and day out, with the task of writing about the nature of space-time, here at last was a truly interesting question. And I wasn't the only one who thought so. Speculation about the first man or woman to find and use a bezoar stone caused a great deal of talk in the magazine office. After all, one does not just pluck a hair ball from the stomach of a goat and plop it in the king's wine. One has to find it, figure out that it's good for something, and then figure out just what that something is.

I discussed with a friend of mine how the discovery might have been made. We understood how folk medicine worked with plants. People were eating plants anyway. They noticed that some of them tasted good, some of them made them sick, and some of them made them want to lie around all day listening to the Doors through headphones. It was obviously very important to remember which was which. But bezoar stones were more problematic. True, people were already eating goats, but whether a bezoar stone is a part of a goat or just *in* a goat is a matter for debate.

Consider the problems of going from the raw material to the fully evolved anti-poison amulet: Suppose the first one was found when somebody at the annual goat-slaughter festival pulled it out of his *tripes au chevrier*. Suppose further that the thing was assumed to have magical or medical powers because it was an anomaly, not explicable by the known laws of digestion. Suppose finally that the goatherds figured that if the gods had put these stones in goats' stomachs, they'd done it for a reason, probably to save the king's life.

Still, somebody had to connect the stone to poisoned wine, and test it. That's where Karl Popper comes in. Karl Popper is a preeminent philosopher of science and it's my experience that he always comes in somewhere if you let him. He and other historians and philosophers of science have discredited the old notion that scientists (and by extension goatherds) proceed by observing and cataloguing facts in an objective fashion until some conclusion about the workings of nature emerges. They've shown that researchers approach their subjects guided by goals, by theory and hypothesis, by available funding.

Funding. Funding is the key to bezoar stones. I didn't recognize it at the time but I've been thinking about bezoar stones now, off and on, for almost ten years. And what I've concluded is that then, as now, research energy was directed to the ailments of people who could afford to pay for a cure. Witness the modern search for a Type A personality antidote. You don't hear a lot about people in the Third World dying of Type A personalities. You know how many calories per day it takes to have a Type A personality? Similarly, in the old days, nobody was slipping arsenic into goatherds' wineskins. It was the potentates who were suffering the poisoning pandemic. This brought a constant stream of goatherds (and everyone else) to the palaces, hawking various herbs, powders, and goat parts as antipoison charms, and hoping for gold. One of them got lucky. Others were not so fortunate. I have to believe that peer review in those days was tougher than it is now, that when a man walked into a potentate's court and said, "Your Highness, my amulet will protect you from poison," the standard response was not to send his paper out for comment, but to chain him to the table, give him a cup of poisoned wine, and ask for a demonstration.

It was this kind of thinking that enabled me to solve the bezoar stone problem—maybe. But it also led me astray. Once you start spending your time with potentates and amulet salesmen it's hard to go back to disulfide bonds. You get an inkling of life beyond spiral galaxies (I say this metaphorically; in actuality I've never had any contact with beings outside of our own particular spiral galaxy), and you want to see more. It was just an inkling, of course. I had no idea at first where the fascination with what we might call hairball science would lead me. It (the inkling) needed a few more years of serious science writing and then a few more years of less serious science writing finally to accrete, like hair in a ruminant's stomach, into the collection you hold in your hands. But accrete it did. And now here it is, twenty-eight pieces on science, and not a spiral galaxy in the bunch.

I can't take full credit for the book, nor would I want to. As with any undertaking of this magnitude, there are a number of people other than myself who deserve thanks and recognition.* My parents not only brought me into the world, they sent me to college, in the hope that one day I would do something worthwhile. Perhaps one day I will. After them, there's Gil Rogin. By jumping to him I have, it's true, skipped over the many teachers who influenced my writing, but none of them actually paid me. Several years ago Gil Rogin took a chance and asked me to write, for money, a column in *Discover,* the magazine in which these pieces appeared from 1985 to 1987 (some in slightly different form than they are here). He is, I suspect, the only editor who would send a writer to southern California to

---

*Will Cuppy, for instance. I adopted the habit of reckless footnoting in shameless imitation of Cuppy's funny pieces on scientific subjects.

interview the manufacturers of toilet-tank fill valves. Of course, I'm probably the only writer who would go. Thank you, Gil.

Thanks also to Marilyn Minden, without doubt the world's best copy editor, who protected and improved these pieces, to Arnold Roth, who illustrated them in the magazine, and did the cover of this book, and to everybody in the *Discover* copy room, who, when I was paid by the word, put squeezes on my columns to get the highest possible word count for the space I was allotted. Tom Dworetzky (and on occasion Sally Dorst and Allan Chen) checked the few facts I was forced to include in my columns, thus keeping me out of court (so far). My agent, Kris Dahl, figured out how to sell the pieces yet a second time, and my editor at Viking, Dawn Seferian, had the enormous good taste to buy them and put them in book form. She has promised me that as a result of this collection I will become more famous than I am now. I have no doubt that she's right.

Following tradition, I have left the best until last—my two most important editors, my wife, Kate, and my friend and fellow writer Richard Liebmann-Smith. Both heard or read most of these pieces before they were finished, and both offered valuable editorial (and other) advice. Richard has helped me with my writing for many years, sometimes to the point of giving me jokes and titles. It was with him that I first discussed the whole bezoar stone problem. Over all this time his critical judgment has been, with one egregious exception, unerring, and his generosity with his time quite amazing. Since I have never responded well to criticism of any sort, both Kate and Richard may, at times, have viewed their task as a thankless one. I have now proved them wrong.

Of course, with all this help, all these people who've had some part in putting me where I am today, there is still, as every writer (and every reader of introductions) knows, somebody who has sole and final responsibility for what goes down on paper . . . and it's not me. No sir. If I have to share responsibility for the good stuff, I'm not going to eat the errors. The funny parts are mine, all right, but if there's anything wrong with any of these pieces it's Richard Liebmann-Smith's fault.

James Gorman
May 1987

The MAN *with* NO
ENDORPHINS

In Praise of the Pump

A momentous event—well, an event, anyway—has occurred in the world of science—well, of toothpaste, to be precise. The dentifrice industry, long represented in most homes by tubes of toothpaste squeezed in infuriatingly incorrect fashion by other members of the household, has now come up with its version of the better mousetrap: the toothpaste pump.

Actually there are several versions, from Check-Up, Colgate, Crest, and Aim. In the past year the companies that make these brands (respectively, Minnetonka, Colgate-Palmolive, Procter & Gamble, and Lever Brothers) have brought out sleek-looking toothpaste pumps, shaped like small, blunt-tipped rockets, as an alternative to the old-fashioned tube. All except Procter & Gamble (which early in the year was still testing the Crest pump in Maine, flying, so to speak, in the teeth of New England conservatism) have their product on drugstore shelves. And, by the companies' accounts, all their pumps are doing very well.

This isn't the sort of news that can be reported objectively, the way one might report the fact that a bubble memory for computers has been perfected, or that someone has discovered that the universe is twenty billion years old. Those are neutral stories. They may be interesting, or even

1

important, but except for the man who has the patent on the bubble memory, or the woman who will get the Nobel Prize for figuring out the age of the universe, people who wake up the morning after the news hits the front page won't find their world changed.

But when someone wakes up and finds, not a tube, lying crumpled, encrusted, and topless on the lip of his sink, reminding him of his slovenly housekeeping and, if he is an introspective person, of his own mortality, but a pump—vertical, cylindrical, clean, upright, unsullied by leaking dentifrice, making him feel, if not immortal, then at least like someone who has a good handle on both dental and domestic hygiene—his life may be permanently changed.

You can see my bias. I'm admittedly pro-pump, partly because I'm a sloppy tube-squeezer. Neat tube-squeezers are generally anti-pump, since, in my opinion, they're already obsessively squeaky-clean in their habits and don't need technological help. But there are other, more objective reasons to praise the pump. It represents the best kind of invention. It's non-electronic. It doesn't have to be programmed. It's not turbo-charged. It is, like the nutcracker and the can opener, a "low-tech" invention.

I'm aware that "low-tech" isn't a common scientific term, like entropy or lymphocyte, so I'll try to define it by example. These things aren't low-tech: the space shuttle, cellular phones, and personal pulse monitors. These things are: steel wool, scissors, ball-point pens, staplers, and the Veg-O-Matic. More generally, a low-tech invention makes no noise and requires no maintenance. It's undemanding, and it usually fits in a drawer or a medicine cabinet.

I'm not altogether immune to the charms of high-tech consumer goods. I own a computer. There are times when I have lusted in my heart after compact disc players and modular televisions, after a home entertainment center so lavish and complex that it would require not an instruction manual but a pilot. But the truth is that my electronic lust has never approached the intensity of the desire ignited in me by the kind of low-tech wonders advertised on late-night television along with albums of old songs, those magical items that are, mysteriously, "not available in stores"—lint brushes and miracle kits to repair cigarette holes, non-stick frying-pans, choppers, dicers, graters, and peelers. There is a Newtonian, or perhaps even pre-Newtonian, innocence to a well-designed carrot peeler. Poems could be written about good spatulas. Garlic presses, pizza cutters, and, perhaps most of all, those little round-ended, serrated, grapefruit tools should be preserved, if they aren't already, in the Smithsonian Institution. I would argue that there is no greater tribute to the benevolent power of the human imagination than a store full of kitchen utensils.

The spirit of low-tech isn't limited to the kitchen. There are wrenches, ratchets, and ball-peen hammers for people who like that sort of thing. And I discovered a new breed of sock recently, made with a mixture of wool and polypropylene, that actually keeps my toes warm in cold weather. I'm far more grateful for this contribution to human life than I am for my word processor. With warm toes, I could write happily with a quill pen.

Most of these wonderful inventions are commercial in nature, the product of the profit motive and not of a humanitarian concern for my toes or anybody else's. So also with the pump. Its origin lies in a major problem faced by toothpaste science, otherwise known as the billion-dollar-a-year dentifrice industry. That problem is success. Ninety-eight percent of the American people brush their teeth. While it's true that a mere 95 percent do it with toothpaste (the others must use baking soda, or something), that still doesn't leave much room for expansion.

So, in the past, the industry, and various inventors inspired by the importance of tooth-brushing to daily life and the possibility of getting rich, have tried improvements, which, if they had been of any use, might also have counted as low-tech gifts to humanity. They include aerosol cans for toothpaste (they didn't succeed—no doubt because aerosols are, if not high-, at least middle-tech); clear, green, bright red, grey, blue, white, and striped dentifrices; mechanical Tube-Wringers (to get the last squeeze); brushes that come with their own paste in them; a range of ingredients, including fennel, limestone, vitamins A, D, and C, clay, and sea salt; and a list of chemicals too long, confusing, and alarming to report. My favorite among the exotic toothpastes, which I haven't yet tried, but which one unbiased dentifrice reviewer reported "does leave the teeth squeaky clean and the breath gaspingly fresh," is Monkey Brand, from India. It isn't a paste but a black—yes, black—powder.

The pump is a different matter. It's an invention so obvious, so simple, and so potentially lucrative that it was invented by West Germans—or at least some of the pump designs were. In fact, pumps have been common for years in Europe, which clearly leads the U.S. in the dentifrice race. Now that the U.S. has jumped into the competition, American manufacturers are reluctant to discuss the design of their pumps, presumably to keep them out of the hands of the Russians. However, in a free society, toothpaste pump designs, like plans for atomic bombs, can often be retrieved from public documents. After considerable effort, I managed to obtain patent reports on some of the pumps.

There are two general kinds, as near as I can figure it. One uses vacuums and valves (Check-Up and Crest), the other is mechanical (Colgate and Aim). Colgate's pump, for example, is a slightly improved version of a caulking gun. Each time you press on the trigger, a piston moves a short distance up a pole, pushing ahead of it the toothpaste, which emerges onto your brush. The Crest pump, a vacuum-valve type, seems more complex, like an artificial heart operated by finger power. It has an upper chamber, from which the paste emerges onto the brush, and valves to let paste in and out of the chamber. When you push the button, the valve leading back into the body of the pump closes and the one leading to the spout opens. The force that you exert reduces the volume of the chambers, thus squishing out the decay-preventing dentifrice. When you take your finger off the button, the volume increases, the valves change position, and new paste is sucked up into the chamber, ready for the teeth of whoever shares your bathroom.

The pumps work. I have personally tested three of them (Procter & Gamble couldn't find an extra Crest pump to send me, and I couldn't make it to Maine), and I can say that those three all get the toothpaste out. Nothing is perfect, of course. I think that using vacuums and valves is already sneaking up into middle-tech, and Check-Up and Aim have flexible plastic tops that will squish, more or less, if you push on them. (Squishiness reminds me of tubes. It lessens the clean, rigid feeling of good housekeeping you get from the Colgate pump.) The Aim pump also has a little tab that you're supposed to stick back into the spout after each use, which is not in the spirit of low-tech. What I myself found most unsettling in my research is that the top of the Check-Up pump bends way back as you push out the toothpaste. To the consumer, at least this consumer, using that pump feels a bit like breaking the neck of a small animal, which is not the way I like to start the morning.

As a personal choice, I have to go with Colgate, with one reservation. Their instructions show a finger being used to work the pump. They're wrong. The only sensible way to work the pump (I have corroborating opinions on this from other consumers) is with the thumb. Why Colgate couldn't figure this out is beyond me.

Of course, the thumb/finger question is nothing compared to the wars that erupt over how to squeeze a tube. I still say that as inventions the pumps are right up there with the garlic press and the nutcracker. And since their inventors are never going to get Nobel prizes or tenured faculty positions, I would like to provide them with a small measure of fame to go along with the piles of money they already have. In gratitude for cleaning up my sink, and in small recognition of his work for the good of the dentifrice-using portion of humanity, I would like to thank, right here in print, the inventor of the Colgate pump (I can't mention everybody), Alfred von Schuckmann of West Germany. With toothbrush in one hand and "dispenser for, in particular, pasty substances" (U.S. Patent No. 4,437,591) in the other, I salute you.

The DNA of the DAR

I for one am very proud of the Daughters of the American Revolution. That hasn't always been the case. I used to think they were stuffy, and altogether too absorbed in their genealogies, or, looking at it biologically, their genes. I didn't mind their looking after the future of those genes, getting out there in the ecosystem of garden clubs and tea parties and scrapping for the kind of biological and social advantage that would enhance their descendants' chances of survival. It was the excessive looking backward, to their ancestors, that seemed to me biologically useless.

I was wrong. The Daughters may well be stuffy, but their family trees certainly aren't useless. The DAR has brought this point home in its latest project, neither a cookbook nor a monument but a genetic study. In cooperation with the Vanderbilt medical school, the Daughters are using their genealogies to trace, not blue blood, but the inheritance of disease. Questionnaires have been sent out to members as part of the DAR Family Tree Genetics Project, asking them to provide a genealogy covering at least three generations that specifies each person's medical problems, including known genetic disorders as well as other diseases. What the scientists are looking at is, in an indirect way, the DNA of the DAR.

When the project was announced, the president general of the DAR, Sarah King of Murfreesboro, Tennessee, pointed out that it could show patterns of inheritance of disease that would be valuable to the medical profession and the public at large. Taking the high ground, she told the membership, "We foresee this program as a boon, not only for our own families but to mankind as a whole. We are fortunate in that we know from whence we came. Our research will serve as an inspiration to others."

I like a president general who knows how to talk like a president general. Furthermore, I like an organization that doesn't indulge in false modesty. And the Daughters are rightfully proud of themselves for getting involved in a project so important that it makes them not only daughters of revolutionaries but revolutionaries themselves. It suggests what could be a tremendously fruitful connection between the world of science and the world of clubs. There is the potential here to liberate population geneticists from their interminable and tedious involvement with fruit flies, to let them say good-bye to *Drosophila* and hello to the DAR, the Boy Scouts, the National Basketball Association, and the Académie Française.

I hope this is what Mrs. King had in mind when she talked about inspiring others, because that's what comes to my mind—a whole new field of science. Call it organizational genetics, or, better, club genetics. Think of it: instead of laboring over a dissecting microscope, checking flies for plum-colored eyes and curly wings, a researcher could study the inheritance of height in professional basketball players. Of course there would be some problems to overcome. The questionnaires would have to have instructions explaining that the traditional qualitative terms used by fans and sportscasters to describe athletes—tall, really tall, and too tall (as in Ed "Too Tall" Jones, who played pro football, in complete disregard for his nickname)—aren't adequate for science. Researchers need feet and inches, if not centimeters. But the basketball study, it seems to me, would be what a scientist or a betting man might call elegant, particularly since it has the advantage of making season tickets an expense that could legitimately be included in a grant application. And for anyone who has sat through the endless quantitative mumbling of a scientific meeting, the project offers the possibility that, during a presentation at the annual meeting of the American Association for the Advancement of Club Genetics, one of the new breed of researchers, instead of asking for an inscrutable slide of some poor *D. melanogaster*'s chromosomes to illustrate his point, will call out from the podium, "Let's go to the videotape . . ."

One could study not only ancestors but also descendants, doing with the DAR or the NBA what Gregor Mendel did with his peas. What do you get, for instance, when you cross the offspring of a center with the offspring of a guard? A forward? And what about real hybrids? What would be the result of a DAR/NBA cross? Perhaps in the first, or F1, generation, there would be a mix—members of the NRA (National Rifle Association) and the ABA (American Bar Association)—while in the F2 generation the offspring would revert to type, DAR and NBA members wondering how in the world they were born into families devoted to guns and the law.

These are only the most obvious projects. Once the discipline of club genetics begins to flower, researchers will be able to tackle the stickier challenges posed by sociobiologists, who have, at one time or another, suggested that almost any human trait, from sexual preference to religious belief, is written in the genes.* My favorite among the qual-

---

*Much to my disappointment, nobody has suggested that there's a separate gene for each religion, though I suspect that's the case.

ities the sociobiologists have described is altruism. Altruism, of course, is selfless behavior, of the sort the DAR has displayed in conducting its study.

In his book *On Human Nature,* E. O. Wilson of Harvard described two kinds of human altruism, hard-core and soft-core. The first involves sacrificing yourself for a close relative who doesn't pester you for money all the time, and it brings no reward other than the survival of someone who shares your genes. This is, in fact, altruistic. Soft-core altruism, on the other hand, brings some kind of non-genetic benefit, like a medal or reward money or a magazine article praising your organization for its public-spiritedness, and is, at base, selfish. (This constitutes a cynical view of human goodness to which neither I nor, I'm sure, the DAR subscribe.) One of the great benefits of club genetics would be that it would offer researchers the opportunity to do *the* altruism study—a survey of the one organization that more than any other purports to be devoted to good, unselfish acts. How could any scientist resist the chance to publish a paper with the title "The Sociobiology of Altruism in the Boy Scouts of America"?

Americans for Common Sense would be another nice group to study, although I would prefer an organization called Americans *with* Common Sense. I'm sure there's something to be done on WITCH (Women's International Terrorist Conspiracy from Hell), if only to find out whether its members have a genetically determined talent for creating great acronyms. A comparative geneticist might discover what separates the Elks from the Lions. And I would be very grateful if someone would take a close look at the Académie Française. This is the organization that defends French culture (including the famous "choking r," which sets apart the true French accent from all imitations) and admits to its ranks the major French intellectuals, like Claude Lévi-Strauss. This is what I want to know: Is the ability—or for that matter, the desire—to speak French with your lips puffed out and your eyes half closed inherited? And, as a subsidiary but related question, Is there a gene for pomp?

Eventually, thanks to the avant-garde action of the DAR, we should be able to do scientifically what the boards of exclusive clubs have been doing all along on an ad hoc basis—decide what a person is like, genetically and personally, on the basis of his or her club memberships. For instance, a person who belonged to both the DAR and the Académie Française could safely be presumed to be a descendant of General Lafayette and to have two dominant pomp alleles.

I suppose that by then anyone putting comments like these down on paper will have to disclose what clubs and organizations he belongs to. To be fair, and in the spirit of full disclosure, which I support for everyone else, I'll do this now. As may already be obvious, I am not, nor could I be, even if I were a woman, a member of the DAR. I was never a Boy Scout. The groups I do belong to are: the National Association of Science Writers, the Authors Guild, and Trout Unlimited, which, I would like to point out, is an organization for, not of, fish.

Guess What's Coming to Dinner?

I just knew it wasn't wrong to eat meat. I had what you might call a gut conviction. It came over me every time I was in close proximity to rare steak or roast pork rubbed with sage, the fat crinkled and brown from the oven. Braised short ribs with onions acted even more powerfully to make me see the virtue in carnivory. And in the presence of a butterflied leg of lamb riddled with garlic slivers, grilled over charcoal, I began to discover countless reasons why my particular arteries would be spared from the atherosclerotic ravages of good food.

To a skeptic, or a cardiologist, I must sound like a man tempted by adultery who develops a belief in open marriage. Science and medicine have spoken on red meat with one voice, and in much the same tone that Sister Miriam used to talk to the sixth grade at St. Justin's about kissing. It's bad for you. It causes heart attacks, triple bypasses, and the indignity of having to put on jogging shorts and have high school girls laugh at you. And yet a good steak, like a kiss, is hard to turn down. I don't know if the Catholic Church has revised its teachings on puppy love—at a certain point in my life I became more concerned with heart disease than the fine points of necking—but I do know that heretical voices have been raised on the subject of meat in

the *New England Journal of Medicine,* which, if not a medical bible, is at least a catechism.

The voices are those of a physician, S. Boyd Eaton (pro-
nounced eatin') from Emory University in Atlanta, and an
anthropologist, Melvin Konner, author of *The Tangled Wing*
(which isn't about chicken parts). They asked this compel-
ling question: What should we have for dinner? And the
answer, medically speaking, was meat. Examining the diets
and ways of life of prehistoric hunter-gatherers, as well as
modern ones, like the !Kung bushmen, Eaton and Konner
concluded that our species adapted over thousands of years
of evolution to a diet that includes a lot of meat, fruit, and
vegetables, and no grains or dairy products, to say nothing
of Pouilly-Fuissé. Modern hunter-gatherers who eat this
way don't suffer the ailments of television producers, like
heart disease, high blood pressure, diabetes, and some kinds
of cancer. (Of course they aren't television producers.) And
Cro-Magnon man, the father of big-game hunting, although
he had no table manners (actually, he didn't even have
tables), was apparently also healthy.

Now, since our bodies are essentially the same as those
of our ancestors, one can only conclude, with a leap of joy,
that it's time for a guilt-free porterhouse. However (there's
a however in every medical paper just when you get out
the steak knives), the meat hunter-gatherers eat, and ate,
comes from what the authors call "free living" animals,
animals with antlers and fleet feet, and also low levels of
fat (particularly saturated fats) and high amounts of a
chemical suspected to combat atherosclerosis—perhaps on
the basis of its medical-sounding name, eicosapentaenoic
acid. This kind of meat seems to be just as good for you as
bulgur in tofu sauce. Presumably, animals like gazelles that
are always getting scared out of their wits and having to
make those remarkable leaps when a lion or David Atten-
borough pokes his head out of the tall grass just never get

the chance to put on much harmful fat. Fatted cattle, on the other hand, live in fear-free abundance, designed, of course, to fat them. The result is that they give us heart attacks.

There are two possible solutions to this problem. One is to hire a lot of people to go to Kansas City in lion masks and scare beef. The other is more realistic, but not much more. Truly health-conscious people will just have to stop doing exegeses of food labels and learn to hunt. If there's any message to be twisted out of Eaton and Konner's thoroughly sensible paper by unscrupulous exaggeration and oversimplification, it's this: you can have your pork and eat it too, as long as it comes from a wild boar. To me, with my weakness for all parts of the pig (the bacon part, the chop part, the sausage part), the thought is a liberating one, but I'm sure it will upset those more serious about their health. *Vegetarian Times* may not know it yet, but with the publication of Eaton and Konner's paper, the leading edge of the nutritional revolution has shifted from fruitarian extremists to the good ol' boys with gun racks in their pickups.

By rights, venison should take over from Tofutti, hunting camps should be the new health spas, and the thin and the chic should rediscover *cuisine sauvage*. The news should also affect the other segments of the health industry. For example, bird hunting might well replace aerobics—providing both exercise and a healthy meal. But I have my doubts. What would become of Richard Simmons? I don't see him, or his devotees, toting shotguns through soggy thickets after woodcock. And I don't believe Jane Fonda will tote a 30.06 into the wild to bag supper. In fact, most nice people, even if they do eat meat, prefer to have someone else do it in.

Well, there's an alternative, which allows one to experience the benefits of the Free-Living Diet with no moral qualms, but I hesitate to mention it. Actually, that's not true, I've been waiting for a chance to mention it for seven years, ever since I read, in the Spring 1978 issue of the *Co-Evolution Quarterly,* what I can say, without fear of contradiction, is the single weirdest piece of food writing ever to be published in a developed country. The title of the article was "How to Use Road Kills."*

This isn't a joke. The article was completely serious. It included the usual tips on skinning, reviews of past repasts (including a hellbender—a huge, ugly, aquatic salamander), a poem by Gary Snyder about eating road kills (and a good poem at that), and this remarkable observation: "Perhaps you are new to the delights of carrion eating and . . . a little unsure of your judgment in these matters. Just what are the consequences of eating spoiled meat? Apparently there are none if it is sterilized by cooking. According to my research, 'spoilage' is a relative, cultural term."

This may be taking cultural relativism too far, and in the wrong direction, but the drift of the article is sound. Our pre-Cro-Magnon ancestors may have been not hunters but scavengers. They were availing themselves of creatures that had been run over by saber-toothed tigers, not Chevys, but the principle is the same. There's a lot of high-quality, low-fat protein out there on the shoulders of I-80 and somebody in some phylum or other is going to eat it, so it may as well be you. It's certainly not going to be me.

No, although I do care about cutting down on fats, and although modern scavenging has logic and ethics on its side,

---

*As I discovered later, eating road kills is commoner than you might imagine. The writer John McPhee once consumed his portion of a roasted road-killed weasel. He recorded the meal in a 1975 *New Yorker* profile of an unconventional Georgia zoologist named Carol Ruckdeschel, who said that she hadn't bought meat for a year, "except for some tongue."

and may, in fact, be the ultimate response to the throwaway society, I'm afraid I have neither the moral fiber nor the stomach for it. I disappointed Sister Miriam many times, although not as many as I would've liked, and I've never been able to stop eating anything I liked. Besides, I have a long, unrequited desire to own a pick-up truck. Eaton and Konner have set me free. I'm going to resume the Cro-Magnon life, with the aid of four-wheel drive. And when one of my Volvo-driving, leaf-eating friends sees me stopped at a light in my new vehicle, nursing a beer, and raises an upwardly mobile eyebrow, I'll just tip back my John Deere cap, have another swallow, and explain to him, in terms that no health-conscious yuppie could question, that it's O.K.—it's all part of my new diet.

The Implausible
Dream

Pharaoh (on couch): *In the dream I'm in this field, and there are all these kine.*
Joseph: *Kine?*
Pharaoh: *That's right, kine, seven fat ones and seven thin ones. And then the thin ones eat the fat ones. Kine—eating each other. Why would a person dream such a thing?*
Joseph: *What are kine?**

O f course, everyone knows that Joseph wasn't a Freudian analyst. He practiced in a different tradition, one in which people were familiar with kine and what they represented. Joseph didn't look for repressed sexual urges in dreams, because—my authority here is Norman Mailer—repression of urges wasn't in vogue in ancient Egypt. Still, as interpreters of dreams, Joseph and Freud shared the belief that, whether your dreams are telling you that you're a latent foot fetishist or that you should store up a lot of grain for seven years of famine (the thin kine), they're telling you something.

Recently, however, some scientists who study the brain,

*Scientists have since learned that kine are cattle.

where it's now universally agreed that dreams originate, have suggested that dreams are a kind of random mental noise, or perhaps neurological junk the brain is discarding. This is going too far. I don't think there's any question that we could all do with fewer phallic symbols in our dreams, but in these new ideas a cigar isn't even a cigar, just an odd impulse leaping a synapse while we sleep.

Among the leading proponents of this sort of thinking are psychiatrists Allan Hobson and Robert McCarley of Harvard Medical School, who concluded, on the basis of sleep research, that there's a dream generator in the brain stem that causes more or less random firings of neurons. The forebrain—which if not the mind is at least more like it than the brain stem—is then forced to interpret these incoherent signals. This is why dreams are filled with people without pants on, relatives who are giant lobsters, and constantly shifting scenes. The forebrain is in the position of a director who must stage nonsense and make the audience think it's seeing a play, a circumstance Hobson and McCarley argue is as common in neurobiology as it is in the theater.

Another non-Freudian idea has been put forth by two biologists, Francis Crick, the Nobel laureate, and his colleague Graeme Mitchison. They base their hypothesis partly on Hobson and McCarley's work, but say that what's going on during the stimulation of neurons is a "reverse learning" or "unlearning" of stuff that the brain needs to lose to keep running clean. Their notion is that during sleep the brain stem sends out stimuli that stir up the neuronal dust, which the forebrain stuffs into dreams and tosses out. Thus, dreams aren't the royal road to the unconscious but the trash bags of the brain.

If true, this is very disappointing news. But perhaps it isn't true. The theories do seem to run counter to the past experience not only of prophets, but of poets, scientists, and, to take an example close to home, me. Why, if my dreams consist of random noise, are the old girl friends who appear in them my own, and not someone else's? And what conceivable reason could there be for my having spent the past twenty years of my life, off and on, confronting the awful fact (while dreaming) that although I'm on a stage and have just received my cue, I've no idea what play I'm in? Crick says that recurring dreams are those that wake the dreamer and, so, cause him to learn instead of unlearn them. A recurring dream is thus a kind of neurological flypaper, and the brain is compelled to indulge in an endless slapstick routine trying to get it off its fingers.

Maybe. But that doesn't solve the larger and far more interesting problem of Samuel Taylor Coleridge, who claimed to have dreamed the poem "Kubla Khan." I know Coleridge had opium to help him, and I'm sure that does something weird to the neurons. In fact, as I understand it, that's the whole point of opium. Still, Coleridge did have this incredibly rich dream, with not only visual images but accompanying verse:

> *In Xanadu did Kubla Khan*
> *A stately pleasure dome decree:*
> *Where Alph, the sacred river, ran*
> *Through caverns measureless to man*
> *Down to a sunless sea.*

He woke up and wrote down this much, and a bit more, including some gardens, woods and dales, caves of ice, and dancing rocks. Tradition has it that he would have got the whole dream down had he not been interrupted by a stranger from Porlock.

Depending on your taste in poetry you may be disappointed or delighted that Coleridge was interrupted, but whatever your opinion, the thing does have meter, it rhymes, it hardly seems the work of neurons firing away like the proverbial monkeys tapping on typewriters. I suppose you could argue that Coleridge, being a poet, had a highly skilled forebrain that was able to ghostwrite the dream on the basis of scattered neurological impulses, a pleasure dome here, a sacred river there. I might believe this for "A damsel with a dulcimer/ In a vision once I saw," which seems like standard poetic boilerplate, but what about: "But O, that deep romantic chasm which slanted/ Down the green hill athwart a cedarn cover!" You just can't get "athwart a cedarn cover" from random neuron firings, no matter how hard you try.

"Kubla Khan" is a tough one for Hobson and McCarley, but it doesn't necessarily refute the clean-up scheme of Crick and Mitchison, who could claim that this is a poem that was supposed to be forgotten. Let's suppose for the sake of argument that they're right. The brain is like someone in an office—all day long it works, learning things, writing things if it's a certain kind of brain, perhaps doing experiments in organic chemistry if it's another kind. During the course of its work, it accumulates the equivalent of scrap paper, little things with jottings on them that say "Column due in two days" or "Structure of benzene? Cube?" Then after all this hard work, while the day part of the brain is enjoying well-deserved sleep, the night crew cleans up. Here's the problem: How can you trust it to know what to throw out?

Take the case of Friedrich Kekulé, the famous nineteenth-century organic chemist from Germany. For years Kekulé attempted to find the structure of the benzene molecule. Always, he tried to stay awake, for fear of what he might lose in a dream. Then one day, while thinking about benzene—he was always thinking about benzene—he fell asleep and had a dream in which a snake was eating its own tail, forming a ring. In Crick and Mitchison's terms, while the part of Kekulé's brain that actually did organic chemistry was dozing, the cleaning team was rummaging around looking for stuff to throw out. "Snake?" it said. "What's this snake doing here? We're doing benzene, right? Chuck it." Fortunately, Kekulé woke up, snatched the dream out of the trash, and realized that the carbon atoms in benzene could form a similar ring, which, in fact, they do.

That's one way to tell the story. The traditional interpretation of this event, which I hold to, is that Kekulé's brain wasn't cleaning itself out but being creative, and that it meant for him to use the snake dreams to make a name for himself in chemistry. I'm not, of course, a Nobel laureate. I'm not even a laureate. And Hobson and McCarley are both doctors. Furthermore, everything I know about neurobiology you have just read. So it would probably be foolish of me to come right out and say these guys are wrong. Instead, let me just say that if *I'm* wrong and brains *are* throwing away these kinds of ideas, maybe we should find a way to stop them.

The Age of Aquariums

There comes a time in everyone's life to keep fish. Just as there comes a time, later, to sell the aquarium at a garage sale. The second event is always an occasion for celebration, but each person reacts to the first in his own way. The chuck-and-chance-it aquarist* meets his fate lightly—buying a fish, chucking it into the aquarium, and chancing it. Of course, in reality, it's the fish who chances it, which is why these aquarists don't lose sleep over the pH of their water, its hardness or softness, or the fact that *Betta splendens* (known in our house as Danny) has a taste for live tubifex worms.

Then there are those of us who take fish, and life, more seriously, those of us to whom an aquarium brings a burden of ecological responsibility similar to that felt by the head of the Audubon Society, or God. In our five-, ten-, or twenty-gallon tanks there are—in addition to the fish—plants, bacterial diseases, and enough protozoan parasites to support an entire university biology department. The average com-

---

*I've borrowed this phrase from people who don't keep fish, but go fishing. A "chuck and chance it" angler chooses lures with cavalier disregard for their appropriateness. This is simply a different form of disrespect for fish.

munity tank cedes nothing to "Dynasty" or "Dallas" in intrigue and conflict. Different fish seek different habitats, territorial battles occur, and, just as on TV, the big ones eat the little ones. An aquarium offers lessons in ecology, biology, chemistry, and personal space.

I came to fish late in life, when I had an income to support them. I purchased, ostensibly for my daughter, a Siamese fighting fish (the aforementioned Danny, since buried in the yard to incantations of "Bye-bye, Danny, bye-bye, fish"), a bowl, and a book. Bowl, book, and fish aren't the ingredients of some piscine excommunication, but the opposite, baptism. For those of you who don't yet own fish, the book is the purchase to avoid. Mine explained to me that in an unheated bowl my betta would grow sluggish and starve. I needed a heater, and since heaters aren't made for bowls and will stratify uncirculated water, I needed an aquarium and a filtration system, which had to be gentle because bettas like calm water. Of course I also needed plants and an aquarium light. I bought it all. Had I remained unlettered about keeping fish, I would have been satisfied with the bowl, and when the fish died I would have just assumed it was his time to go. Then I would have been able to put dried flowers, or rocks, or little plaster figurines of cocker spaniels in the bowl, and to resume life. With fish, ignorance may not be bliss, but it's cheaper than knowledge.

As happens, one fish led to another, and the aquarium was struck by death and disease; I dosed my fish with tetracycline and malachite green to combat bacterial fin rot and ich (*Ichthyophthirius multifiliis,* a parasitic protozoan). I bought an 800-page compendium on fish and their diseases. And I subscribed to *Tropical Fish Hobbyist,* which revealed to me the lengths to which fish obsession could be taken. The cover of the April issue consisted of eight photographs of different platies (fish). And the explanation of the cover began with this sentence: "What can one say about *Xiphophorus maculatus,* the platy or moon, that hasn't been said a thousand times over . . . ?"

What indeed? And where does one end, once one starts to think, and write, about platies in a certain way? There's the old saying about greener grass, and it's also true, at least in the Free World (this is in fact the foundation of both the Free World and the tropical fish business), that no matter what one has, one always wants more. If you have platies, you want red-tailed sharks; if you have plastic plants, you want living ones; if you have a five-and-a-half-gallon tank with one betta, a black neon, two catfish, and an algae eater named Glom, you want four 1,000-gallon tanks, covering every wall of the living room, which reproduce—exactly—the streams of Southeast Asia, Lake Tanganyika, the Amazon River, and the Great Barrier Reef. I began to see, after reading the advertisements and articles in *Tropical Fish Hobbyist* and monitoring my own rising lust for bigger tanks and weirder fish, that underneath the patina of interest in aquatic biology lies the true passion of the aquarist, a peculiar but intense form of greed. It was clear that I'd chosen the right hobby. And it occurred to me that there was no point in continuing to fool around with pet stores. I should follow my avocation to its ultimate manifestation. I went to Baltimore.

There is no greener grass, pisciculturally, than Baltimore. It's the home of the National Aquarium in Baltimore, which is so big that you don't walk around it, you walk around in it. Its two big tanks are rings, and you're in the hole in the middle of the rings, with fish swimming in circles around you. My aquarium holds five and a half gallons of water and five fish, and cost me, including light, filter, plants, and rocks, about $50. The National Aquarium has a million gallons of water and almost 5,000 fish, and it cost Baltimore about $20 million. If the guy who runs the National Aquarium gets tired of fish, they get rid of him, not the aquarium.

Naturally, I approached the aquarium not as a layman but as an aquarist. So what if its circular Open Ocean Exhibit has 220,000 gallons of water and sand tiger sharks the size of my Volkswagen? It's still an aquarium. For instance, in my tank the betta chases the other fish and will sometimes nip them. The same thing happens at the National Aquarium. One day a brown shark ate a sheepshead and started writhing in indigestion. Attracted by the motion, one of the sand tigers nipped the brown—in a manner of speaking. He eviscerated the smaller shark with one bite. You can argue that retrieving a four-foot disemboweled shark from a tank that still includes his disemboweler is fundamentally different from picking out a battered inch-long black neon from a home tank with your fingertip. And that may be so. A four-foot fish cannot easily be buried in the yard, and it does seem wrong to say "Bye-bye, fish" to a dead shark.*

There are a few other differences. When you feed the sharks, you stand on an unprotected catwalk over their tank and waggle fish on the end of a pole in between their jaws. You don't want to fall in. In feeding my fish, I've experienced a mild ennui, but never outright fear. Then there's the cost of the food. The National Aquarium spends $100,000 a year on krill, lettuce, peas, herring, broccoli, oysters, clams, shrimp, and assorted other forms of fish chow. The aquarium also spends $100,000 a year on salt. The water—plain Baltimore tap water—goes for $25,000 a year.

And there's the filter. Aquarists, by default, must love technology as much as they love fish. An aquarium isn't like a hamster cage, which just keeps the hamster from

*In fact, the National Aquarium doesn't have a yard (that I could see), which may be why they send their dead fish to the University of Maryland pathology laboratory.

escaping to die between the walls and ruin dinner parties. An aquarium maintains creatures from another world; it's like a reverse submarine. And what keeps it going is the filter. For the home aquarium there are under-gravel filters, sponge filters, box filters, outside-the-tank filters, all the kinds of filters you could imagine. But the filtration system of the National Aquarium is to the home filter as the space shuttle is to a paper airplane. There are no plastic tubes in this set-up. I'm talking twelve-inch pipes, 45,000-gallon holding tanks, atomic absorption tests for water quality, mass spectrographs, refractometers, computers, lots of big, big pumps, and two rooms—one huge, with pipes and pumps and tanks painted in bright colors, like the Pompidou Center turned outside in, the other steamy and small, where the water flows over plastic cylinders on which grow bacteria that digest fish waste. I'm talking about a system that circulates all 555,000 gallons of water in the aquarium's two big tanks in only ninety minutes. To put this in terms we can all appreciate, if this system were hooked up to my tank, in an hour and a half it would filter the water, and probably the fish, 100,909 times, approximately.

Maybe this is something that only appeals to those of us who read articles like "Crustaceans in the Home Aquarium (Part 6—Mantis Shrimp and Barnacles)" and wait eagerly for Part 7. Perhaps there exists, somewhere, a person able to stand in the filter room of the National Aquarium and be unmoved. On me the effect was overpowering, and unexpected. I no longer covet a larger tank, for the same reason that mystics who've experienced nirvana don't apply for American Express cards. Once you've seen the Platonic Ur-Aquarium of Baltimore you're forever spoiled for the fifty-five-gallon fully equipped tank and stand now on sale for $144.99 at my pet store (a good deal, even if I am no longer interested in it).

This isn't to say I've abandoned my aquatic fantasies altogether. What happened during my spiritual experience in Baltimore was that I learned that some of the feeding of fishes in the 335,000-gallon Atlantic Coral Reef ring tank is done by scuba divers. I saw them, floating with the fish, petting them, handing out bits of food. I also learned that these divers are almost all volunteers. Inevitably, the following thought occurred to me: If I can persuade my wife and children to move to Baltimore; if I become a certified diver; if I take the special course for volunteers—then, although I may never be able to get a 335,000-gallon aquarium for my living room, I'll be able to get *in* one.

Mother Goose Biology

There's a reason people hit alligators over the head with sticks. It's not genetic. It's cultural. In fact, it's literary. But first the alligator story: About two years ago I was on a nature walk around a pond in the Everglades—looking at egrets, hawks, and roseate spoonbills in the company of people who said things like "The common egret has black feet; it's the *snowy* egret that has *yellow* feet, sweetheart." We happened to pass by a big alligator and the level of the conversation took a sudden drop. (The same people said things like "That's a *big* alligator.") The ranger leading the walk told us that the year before she had come on a young woman beating a similar-sized alligator over the head with a stick. The alligator hadn't eaten the woman's dog, or bitten off the hand or foot of a loved one. The woman liked the alligator. She was just trying to get it to open its mouth so her boyfriend could get a good picture.

Next Ernest and Celestine: They are, respectively, an adult male bear and a young female mouse who share an apartment in a city I take to be Paris. (There is an alligator connection here.) They appear in several children's books by Gabrielle Vincent, which I bought for my daughters. The Ernest and Celestine books are very sweet, but, biologically

28

speaking, there's something horribly wrong with them. I don't mean the fact that a bear and a mouse live together in an apartment. What I'm talking about is the fact that they are a bear and a mouse. What is their relationship? One might think at first, since Ernest is very fatherly, that they are members of the same family, or at least of the same species. My sixteen-year-old nephew made this assumption when he started to read one Ernest and Celestine story to my older daughter. Then he became completely confused by the drawings. "I don't know," he said of Celestine. "It looks an awful lot like a rat to me."

His comment was what opened my eyes (I didn't figure all this out by myself). I realized, in a way that I hadn't before, that she was a rat—or a mouse, anyway. Why wasn't she a bear? Who was Ernest? Then I thought of the song about the fly marrying the bumblebee (the ultimate interfaith marriage), of all the stories in which squirrels, rabbits, cats, and foxes peacefully co-exist, and, by what seemed to me inexorable logic, of that woman smacking the alligator. Kids' books did it to her. That was my conclusion. She hadn't just assumed that all of Florida was part of Disney World— a common enough mistake. She was the victim of countless silly children's stories (some purveyed by Disney, to be sure) that had turned her sense of the natural world upside down. Maybe she didn't believe that the alligator was a postman who was married to Rosie Spoonbill, the village gossip. Maybe. But she didn't believe it would bite her either.

And no wonder, if she was brought up on the books my children read. Think of what Ernest and Celestine do to biology. If it were just the two of them, that would be O.K. All species have eccentrics. But their world is infested with adult bears and young mice in family units. When Ernest and Celestine visit a more established household (they themselves live in reduced circumstances), we don't suddenly see little baby bears running around, or Mama and

Papa Mouse. We see two adult bears, male and female, presumably married, and a brood of mice for Celestine to play with. Children? Are we supposed to believe that the mice are the bears' children? Or is some odd kind of symbiosis going on—interspecific foster care? If so, when the mice leave their children on the doorsteps of bears, how do they steal away the cubs? Perhaps (I haven't read every Ernest and Celestine book, so I can't be sure) Gabrielle Vincent has constructed a world like that of H. G. Wells's *The Time Machine,* in which ugly underground people, the Morlocks, create a comfy world for pretty, childlike, above-ground people, the Eloi, whom they eat. Could it be that the mice aren't the bears' children, but their snacks?

As any parent knows, the Ernest and Celestine stories aren't the only "alligator beaters" (as these books are called in the trade, or should be) on the market. Another remarkable series is produced by Richard Scarry, the James Michener of kidlit. Richard Scarry dispenses more information per page than any other children's author. I think his books look cluttered, like a house too full of knickknacks, but children, perhaps because they have so much room on their mental shelves, love them. In all his books, all animals pal around with all other animals. A family of cats has, as a friend, a worm, who, in a triumph of impossibility that even I find irresistible, wears a shirt, a pant, and a shoe. (He ties his own shoelace, which I leave for you to imagine.) The classic Richard Scarry scene has a fox, a rabbit, a dog, and a cat enjoying themselves, with no interspecific conflicts, on the same swing set. I suppose it's pointless to complain that his creatures (except for the worm) are so denatured that they have no identities and have become interchangeable cuddlies. But when he puts a lady pig in a butcher shop slicing baloney, and hanging next to her is a ham—that's sick.

In the sea of happy furriness that greets the parent shopping for kids' books, one volume is *hors de classe,* if not *sui generis* (it's hard to tell with these foreign languages) in its sins against taxonomic integrity. The book is *Stuart Little,* by E. B. White. There is no simple matter of cats taking earthworms for car rides. In *Stuart Little* a human family gives birth—or perhaps I should say gives rise, since this is more like speciation than reproduction—to a mouse. (Presumably this story was the inspiration for Ernest and Celestine.) The Littles (who are actually full size) take the mouse to their bosom, being careful not to crush him, and he becomes a valued, if small, member of the family. I can't say it's not a good story. I ended up rooting for the mouse, as I'm sure everyone does. But I can't help wishing that Mr. Little, when he was first presented with a rodent in swaddling clothes, had been as honest as my nephew, and had said to the nurse, or Mrs. Little, or whoever was around, "I don't know, it looks an awful lot like a rat to me."

It's not so much anthropomorphism that I'm opposed to. I like a good talking duck as well as the next daddy. I just want the duck to be a duck, not a Smurf in feathers. It's not an impossible trick. Beatrix Potter carried it off, with foxes and rabbits as well. In one of her stories, Jemima Puddle-duck is bamboozled by a smooth-talking fox into providing the fixings for her own roasting, but is saved by the farm's collie dog and two foxhounds. This is no biology text—the fox talks—well—and he even has a kitchen, or some place to roast his ducks before he gobbles them up. But look at the personalities of the animals. The fox is unscrupulous. The duck is an idiot. The collie is a responsible sort, and the foxhounds are enthusiastic, but not too bright. Enhancing the realism, the foxhounds, once they save the duck, eat up all her eggs.

Mother Goose also contains some sound animal stories. Three blind mice getting their tails cut off with a carving knife may be bloody and a bit surreal, but it's nowhere near as bizarre as *Stuart Little*. And when Little Miss Muffet is scared off her tuffet, I think no student of either children or spiders could object. (We'll let the whole matter of what, exactly, a tuffet is rest for now.) Furthermore, the stories that do justice to animals also do better by the human beings that I assume the animals are supposed to represent.* Aesop, though not usually thought of as a children's writer, could well be used to give young people a solid grounding in both animal and human behavior. In one of my favorite fables, a wolf tries to convince a lamb that it has done something wrong, and should therefore be eaten. The lamb correctly and skillfully argues its innocence. Then the wolf decides to stop wasting its time and says, "Well, you may be a pretty slick talker, but I'm going to eat you anyway." I've had similar exchanges with editors.

Finally, there are the tales collected by the Brothers Grimm, which are satisfyingly full of the duplicity, hunger, and violence that characterize life in the woods, the playground, and the office. The best may be Red Riding Hood, if you read the Grimms' tale and not one of the watered-down versions in which the wolf merely scares the grandmother and the girl. According to the Brothers Grimm, the wolf eats both of them. They're liberated when a huntsman slits the beast open, then fills him with rocks and sews him back up. And the grandmother isn't brought trifling sweets, but a cake and a bottle of wine, a gift that would be more to the taste of the grandmothers I know. A lot has been written about this story, and I'm not going to start a new analysis of the psychosexual currents running beneath its

---

*This brings up the question of why so few books for children are about actual, unfurred people (*Homo sapiens sapiens*). I suspect the reason is that even the smallest child knows from personal experience that there are limits to the sweetness of even the nicest adult of its own species. On the other hand, kids will believe anything you tell them about bears and mice.

surface. I like it because it contains a wonderful poetic statement of the workings of evolution. We all know that natural selection forged the wolf's teeth into tools to rend and tear flesh. But that's a ponderous way to say it. How much more felicitous to have the wolf himself declaim, in response to Red Riding Hood's innocent wonder (the ultimate source of all scientific inquiry), "The better to eat you with, my dear." Darwin himself must have loved that line.

The Urge for Going

There is a famous goose song called "The Urge for Going." Joni Mitchell wrote it and Tom Rush sang it (he probably still does) huskily, sometimes not quite on key. In it, Canada geese appear as romantic figures, as they do in most goose music. They fly in V-formation in the crisp autumn air, and their flight, squarely in the tradition of the elegiac goose lyric, is a symbol of change, of loss, of wanderlust. We all know these geese—going south, going north, always going somewhere. These are what we call songwriter's geese.

They are not, however, representative of all Canada geese. Some of the others waddle along on the ground with an air of utter pragmatism. And honk. Unmelodiously. Loudly. When Felix, in "The Odd Couple," clears his sinuses, the noise he makes isn't precisely the same as that made by a waddling Canada goose, but it has precisely the same amount of charm. These other geese will fly if they have to, but only to avoid freezing or starving to death. If they get the chance to trade their long migratory past for a park pond and white bread year-round, they snap it right up with their greedy little bills.

Some of these geese have moved to Greenwich, Connecticut, a town that is near the top of the list on all three of the important criteria for residential real estate—location, location, and location. It has vast lawns, parks, ponds, a high demographic profile, and Long Island Sound. It never gets too hot or too cold, and the roughly 5,000 geese that have settled there apparently blithely ignore the whispers around town that they aren't Republicans. Of course, the truth is that there are Democrats in Greenwich, and not all of them are geese. And although many people in Greenwich don't like the geese, this has nothing to do with politics or social standing. It's the kind of reason that never gets into goose songs. Droppings. Five thousand geese can drop a lot of droppings on the beach, the estate, and the fourteenth green. And when they do—that, if you'll pardon the expression, is when the scat hits the fan.

Greenwich recently hit the newspapers and the evening news because of its goose droppings. It had gotten to the point where the park department had to borrow the yacht club's ceremonial cannon to shoot blanks to scare the birds off the beaches. Even the CBC (Canadian Broadcasting Corporation) called town officials for a radio interview. What they wanted to know was why these "Canada" geese weren't coming home.* The flocking instinct of journalists is well known, and I saw no reason not to follow in everyone else's path (being careful where I stepped, of course). I went first to Byram Park, one of the places the geese frequent. It's a nice park—almost as nice as the property around some of the town's middle-range houses. The geese were there, on the grass of the ball field. They were also in Bruce Park, near the tennis courts, repetitively bobbing their heads up and down as they plucked the grass (geese, like buffalo, are grazers). They were pretty, with their black necks and that splash of white on their cheeks (I'm not sure that geese

*A sign, I take it, that at least some Canadians are starting to take themselves less seriously.

have cheeks in the strict scientific sense of the word, but I don't know what else you'd call them). And they were pleasant to watch. But—I don't want to be coy about this, so I'll say it straight out—there was goose doo all over the place.

If it were only Greenwich, only Greenwich would care. But these stay-at-home geese aren't just a few renegades. There are nonmigrating geese all over the country. They're moving into the parks and onto the golf courses and lawns. They're precipitating an environmental crisis of unique proportions, a competition for habitat (and nice habitat at that) that could be the severest test yet of America's love of wild creatures. Among the places afflicted with nonmigrating geese are Massachusetts, Connecticut, New York, New Jersey, Pennsylvania, Virginia, Minnesota, and the cities of Seattle, Denver, Cleveland, Nashville, and Toronto. (Some of the geese have stayed in Canada.) Minnesota has an urban goose population of about 30,000 to 40,000. Connecticut and New York have about 10,000 between them.

What has happened is that instead of going back and forth from Canada to the South (back and forth, back and forth—I'm sure the geese hated it), some pioneering birds found climates where it never got too hot or too cold, and where there were lawns to eat, and, even better, people to feed them. Now, according to Kathryn Converse of the U.S. Fish and Wildlife Service, these nonmigrating geese hop from park to estate, looking for new nesting sites as their population grows. This is how one gets geese: Two geese stop in the yard in the spring, checking out your pond as a place to raise children. Two geese in the yard look cute. As everyone knows, the natural food of geese is stale bread, so you give them some. In Greenwich, maybe you have the cook buy an extra baguette for the birds. They eat. They stay. They reproduce. More geese. More cuteness. More goose poop. In three years there are fifty geese—permanent geese that don't even know where Canada is—and everyone in the neighborhood is wearing rubber boots.

Converse, who provided me with most of this information—I am not, personally, a goose expert—knows quite a bit about geese. She did her Ph.D. thesis on nonmigrating geese in Fairfield County (Connecticut), where Greenwich is, and neighboring Westchester County (New York). She saw the human misery firsthand—houses where people had to have two sets of shoes (two complete sets of shoes!) because of slippery grass. Ornamental ponds where the water had turned green—and I don't mean the emerald green of the Caribbean, I mean goose-doo green. She followed geese around—1,000 individually marked geese—for three years. And she got to know them and their desires. Geese like water to land in and sleep on because while they're on it they can see predators coming. They like grass to eat, particularly short grass, because the new shoots have the most protein. They like to nest on islands or peninsulas. They like water that doesn't freeze in the winter, or doesn't stay frozen for long periods, like the bays of Long Island Sound. And they love people who feed them. If you were to design the ideal wildlife management area for geese—it would be Greenwich. Geese, in other words, like exactly the same environment people do, and since they don't have to buy houses or pay taxes, they can live wherever they want.

You might think that when the geese get to be too much, you can just run them off the property. And it is possible to get rid of geese, but it's not easy. First, never feed them. Then, make sure nobody else within a mile of you feeds them. Build barriers around the ornamental ponds (forget what they look like). Finally, harass the geese, incessantly. Persistence is the key. Nastiness and meanness of heart are also useful. Converse says that in the course of her research she would find one golf course with geese, and

another with none. The goose-free course would have achieved
its idyllic state by having employees on golf carts charge
into flocks, shouting unfriendly things at the birds, every
day. Geese, when they know they aren't wanted, won't stay.
The difficulty is in convincing them that you don't want
them.

It is this obtuseness, this complete failure by geese to
take a hint, that's bound to drive goose-ridden communities
to violence. The current balance, with the geese happy and
the people unhappy, can't last. The birds have been smart
enough so far to settle in residential areas where there's
no goose season. But the nation that taught the passenger
pigeon and the buffalo their lessons isn't going to let the
fish and game laws stand in its way. I see a lot of 12-gauges
coming down from a lot of attics and snuggling against a
lot of homeowners' shoulders. I see a lot of intentional disregard of the Migratory Bird Act of 1918. I see a lot of
Labrador retrievers that have spent their lives chasing tennis balls and getting squished between suitcases in the back
of station wagons finally getting the chance to retrieve real,
dead geese—by the thousands.

Nor will the geese be the only victims. And this is the
real tragedy—the birds are going to spoil it for all the other
animals. I'll explain why. First, I think we can assume, *a
priori,* that there are huge numbers of people whose love
for other living creatures is founded on song lyrics. Seeing
or hearing about other creatures at a distance, given the
right chord progression, can make one inordinately fond of
them. Because the average lover of wild things doesn't know
the objects of his affection intimately, it's easy to spring to
their defense. Take coyotes—they eat the odd pet here and
there, but they haven't made a habit of it. Maybe they do
eat lambs, but then you know those shepherds, always crying
"Coyote!" As for grizzlies, there's no doubt that they kill
people, but I've detected, in conversations with the ecolog-

ically sensitive, a suspicion that they don't kill *good* people. They kill people who sleep in the wrong places, or carry salamis into the woods, or use deodorants and perfumes in Glacier National Park. Like test pilots, lovers of nature feel that there's a kind of hikers' right stuff that will see you through your confrontations with the natural world. (Most of the potentially anti-grizzly hikers, are, of course, already dead.)

As for the other wildlife one is likely to encounter between Greenwich and Wall Street, pigeons tend to stick to public buildings and statues, and although raccoons will steal your garbage, they don't mess around with your lawn. Rabbits are sensitive to insults. And rats—well, rats go after renters. But geese, geese are birds of a different feather. And once you get to know a goose, up close and personal, it's difficult ever again to get misty-eyed about the wonders of nature. An animal that makes that incredibly nasal noise, that's primarily interested in its own comfort, and that would rather live on handouts than migrate for a living is clearly no better than a human being. If that's true of one wild creature, it's probably true of the whole lot. You see the inevitable conclusion: If they (all other living things) are no better than we are, and if it comes down to a fight over the same lawn—*Blam!*—or pond—*Blam!*—or national park—*Blam! Blam!*—why shouldn't we be the ones to get it?

The Sign of the RAM

I have just had my horoscope done by a computer program. This wasn't an experiment in artificial intelligence. I wasn't asked to read a sheet of paper that informed me that I was "a free spirit" and to determine whether this bit of wisdom had come from a person or a computer. That would have been an impossible test, since all horoscopes read as if they were written by computers. I simply bought a computer program called Deluxe Astro-Scope, plugged in my date, time, and location of birth (latitude and longitude were required—no Mickey Mouse here), and waited while the disc drives whirred, Alan Turing* turned over in his grave, and the printer spewed forth ten pages of planets, aspects, midheavens, and modalities. It even told me, in a roundabout way, my sign— Taurus.†

---

*Turing, whose sign was Cancer, was an early theorist of artificial intelligence.
†What the computer didn't tell me, but I knew anyway, was that there is a homonym for my sign, "torus," the term in solid geometry for the doughnut shape. This fact has given me a perverse yearning to dress up as a glazed doughnut, walk into a California singles bar frequented by mathematicians, and say to some blonde who looks as if she knows her solid geometry, "Hi, I'm a torus."

The printout contained an enormous amount of exotic information that's no doubt of great value to the professional astrologer. I can now tell you that my Neptune is in House Twelve, my moon in conjunction with Mars, my Jupiter in Aquarius—and my bill is $295—for the floppy disc and accompanying documentation. Insight isn't cheap. The program provided me with some startling pronouncements on my character. It said, for instance, "You have an unyielding nature, which makes it very difficult for those with alternate opinions to co-exist with you." This, of course, is absolute nonsense.

Mine isn't the only astrology program; it's one of many. Depending on your point of view, computers have invaded astrology, or astrology has invaded computers. There are at least two companies devoted to astrological programs: AGS Software of Orleans, Massachusetts, from which I purchased Deluxe Astro-Scope, and Matrix Software of Big Rapids, Michigan. The emphasis in their catalogues is on professional astrology. In the Matrix brochure a headline trumpets "Make money with your home computer!" And AGS notes that "you can make Electronic Astrologer Astro-Reports consistent moneymakers in a horoscope calculation service." That's not why I ordered the program, but I was glad to hear it. If the writing business goes sour, I'll be more than happy to tell you (to borrow the typography of the printout) whether your horoscope is dominated by FIRE, EARTH, AIR, or WATER—for a small FEE.

The programs Matrix and AGS offer can do almost anything. With them you can not only cast an individual horoscope but also check the compatibility of two people, do astrological research, biorhythms, numerology, and tarot readings. You can even do a little sexual astrology for consenting adults. The brochure from AGS touts their Deluxe Sex-O-Scope as providing "a playful, witty, R-rated description of romantic and lovemaking styles and preferences.

Does not include explanatory pages—these we leave to your ingenuity!"

My mother warned me about people who combined sexual innuendo and exclamation points, so it was with some trepidation that I called AGS about the program I wanted. I needn't have worried. My conversation with the woman who answered was thoroughly official. Instead of asking, alluringly, "What's your sign?" she said, "What's your operating system?" I wish I could say that when I answered "CPM" she said, "Ah, you're business oriented, a pioneer, with a large library of free software," but she didn't. She asked me about my RAM, not Aries, the sign of Bismarck and J. P. Morgan, but Random Access Memory—that RAM, the sign of Stephan Wozniak and Steven P. Jobs.

As to the program she sent me, I can't fault it. It provided better, or at least more, advice than I ever got from the newspaper. At times it appeared incredibly perceptive, as when it pointed out that I was "courageous and daring." Then it would go ludicrously off the mark, describing me as "vain and lazy." Still, it was nice to have the feeling that someone was taking an interest in me, talking to me, about me, even if he was saying nasty things. The astrological second person ("You are tall, dark, and handsome," "You will become amazingly wealthy, today") is irresistible in its illusion of intimacy, whether it comes from a computer, a newspaper column, or an astrologer in the flesh. Even when you know perfectly well that a million other people are reading "You are a deeply passionate person who needs endless love—from lots of different people," it can still feel as if someone has finally understood you.

The only problem with astrology is that it's all hooey. I didn't make this up just to be mean. I got it out of the *Encyclopædia Britannica,* to which I often turn for guidance when I'm not reading my horoscope. The encyclopædia said, in a tone I thought was a bit harsh, that after Newton astrology became "scientifically untenable" and, in the West, "more and more fraudulent." It called it a pseudoscience and said, "Modern Western astrology, though of great interest sociologically and popularly, generally is regarded as devoid of intellectual value." In other words—hooey. What, then, does it mean for the culture as a whole that computers are being put to uses "devoid of intellectual value"? I think it's very good news.

The advent of computerized astrology marks the intrusion of silliness into the halls of science. The computer is the closest most of us get to a scientific advance. It's an electronic icon, the reigning trinket of twentieth-century technology. It's one thing to use such a device to pretend you're commanding the Starship *Enterprise* and trying to crush the Klingon Empire (at least that's *science* fiction). But it's another to force the computer to play handmaiden to the occult, to irrationality and superstition. That's a scandal, an outrage. As Henry Higgins would say: How simply frightful! How humiliating! How delightful!

It's not that I rejoice in seeing the poor computer dragged in the mud of the zodiac. It's just that I've been worried by dire predictions that computers will dehumanize us, that they'll take over our lives, suck the juice out of them, and leave us nothing but bits and bytes. Computer astrology seems to put the lie to these claims. Astrology may be dumb, but it's human. If even science writers are sitting around forcing computers to do silly, irrational, and useless things like cast the astrological charts of Prince Charles and Howard Cosell,* then we are as likely to end up dominated by the chill, restrictive logic of the computer as a Taurus is to change his mind.

---

*Prince Charles, a Scorpio, has "a preference for rich, elegant surroundings & possessions" (sic). Cosell, an Aries, is "quite tolerant of others' faults," as everyone knows.

One has to remember, when considering the potential dehumanizing effect of computers, that being human isn't always such a noble thing. Part of being human may be caring for families and friends, reading (or writing) great literature, and going to India to help Mother Teresa. It is, however, equally, if not more, human to bet on horses, philander, read your horoscope, play games, and try to make money by selling astrology programs. All these activities, and others, remain possible, if not easier, with computers. There are programs to handicap horses, keep bowling scores and averages, do biorhythms, throw (or perhaps I should say compute) the I Ching, and teach you how to win at blackjack. There's Deluxe Sex-O-Scope. On the same machine you can go shopping, trace your family tree to Prince Charles (or Howard Cosell), and send electronic love notes to compatible computer owners. And there are the games, from Space Invaders to Bible Baseball. In one catalogue of software for Apple computers there are two pages of general science and more than forty pages of games. Obviously, computers aren't turning people into humdrum machines. People are turning computers—as they have every other bit of technology, from the internal combustion engine to the machines (I know they exist, even though I've never seen one) that make rubber dinosaurs—to their own frivolous and irrational pursuits.

It's true that I'm only talking about home computers, so I don't want to wax overly optimistic. Until we get the computers at the Pentagon and the Kremlin I-Chinging and doing horoscopes for every person that ever lived, we're not really safe. But there are teenage hackers who can set that up for us. And if you can't abide astrology, think of it this way: a computer that's busy worrying about the difference between Gemini and Virgo isn't fooling around with your bank account.

Remember, these words come to you from "a perfection-ist" with "a deep and inquiring mind" who, although he "loves practical jokes" and has "a tendency to be shallow," is nonetheless graced with "cool logic." I couldn't have put it better myself.

There's This Tribe . . .

M y wife, when she was studying psychological theory, would often come home and regale me with stories of how a child's upbringing could damage his psyche—breast-feeding to age twelve causing uncontrollable eye twitching, or toilet training with rewards of M&Ms leading to idiopathic colitis each Halloween. Being naturally argumentative, I always tried to come up with a counterexample. Well, I would say, the !Kung Bushmen of the Kalahari breastfeed until the midlife crisis—the child's—and there's nothing wrong with them. And what, I would ask, did she have to say about the Yanomamö of South America? I happened to know that they didn't celebrate Halloween, nor did they have M&Ms—let alone toilets.

It could be that our arguments on matters of human nature were the result of my own severely flawed personal character. But I don't think so. I blame the fights on anthropology. In no branch of knowledge is it so true that having a little of it can be a dangerous thing. And I know of no other field where so many know so little about so much. Some of us use our knowledge responsibly. I tend to use my own vast store of information on the Gururumba to speak for the dignity and diversity of all that is human. Other people, from what I can see, use the little crumbs of information they've garnered from Anthro 101 to make trouble in what would otherwise be pleasant conversations.

We all have our favorite tribes, peoples who can be thrown up to devastate a conversational opponent who thinks he has just explained why men (or women) are genetically designed to take out the garbage. "Ah," you say, "but among the Gazonga there is no garbage!" The classic choices are the !Kung, the Ik, and the people who stretch their lips out with little round discs (which I've always thought were distressingly reminiscent of clay pigeons). This trio is known, at least to me, as the good, the bad, and the ugly.* But there are many other possibilities, like the Hopi, the Pygmies of the Ituri forest, the Kwakiutl, the Inuit, the Yir Yoront, not to mention cross-cultural studies.† If you missed anthropology in college, you needn't fear that you'll lack examples. Public television recently ran a Tribe of the Week series (it was actually called "Disappearing World"), allowing their upwardly mobile audience to get acquainted with peoples who were headed in the other direction. (I think it's fair to say that disappearing from the face of the earth is the *ne plus ultra* of downward mobility.) I'm convinced that somewhere in the world there's a tribe for every point of view.

If you'd like to argue in favor of adultery, for instance, you're in good shape. Sex has always been a mainstay of anthropology. We do have it in our own culture, but it always seems better in places like Micronesia. Variety is the spice not only of life but of ethnography. I suggest you read

*The !Kung are the hunter-gatherers who treat their children well and make no mortgage payments. The Ik are the people who degenerated into pure selfishness when faced with starvation. The clay pigeon people are familiar to anyone who has ever looked through any copy of *National Geographic*.
†Who could resist the comparison of the Machiguenga, of the Amazon rain forest, with the Parisians, of France?

Ulithi: A Micronesian Design for Living by William A. Lessa, published in 1966, which I found in a carton of my wife's old books from college. There is an unclothed girl on the cover, and if you zip directly to chapter seven, "Sexual Behavior" (I had to do it, I was researching this column), you'll find an account of the holiday of *pi supuhui*. This Ulithian phrase is loosely translated as "a hundred pettings." The idea behind the holiday is that each person pairs off with somebody of the opposite sex and heads for the bushes. Spouses can't pick each other. The best part about *pi supuhui* to my mind is that it's not set for any specific day. It's held whenever anyone suggests it. I envision the Ulithians calling for *pi supuhui* in much the same way that undergraduates shout "Food fight!"

Sometimes it's hard to figure out what point of view a tribe is meant to support. The Jalé of New Guinea are cannibals (or were, as late as the 1960s) who clamped the eyelids and lips of their victim (or meal) shut with bat wing bones so the soul wouldn't get out and give them indigestion. Although the Jalé had some religious reasons for the way they treated their enemies up to the point where they were well done, the reason they ate them was not sacred but profane. People taste as good as or better than pork. I guess the Jalé could come in useful sometime in an argument about who has—or is—the best barbecue.

There are two ways to look at argumentative anthropology. You can use it, or you can deplore it. I favor using it, which means you should try to be the first one in a conversation to bring up a primitive people. This gives you a definite edge. If your opponent (I confess to viewing all conversations as contests of one sort or another) is first, he has the advantage. You are put in the position of a poker player responding to a bet: "I'll see you your circumcision rite and raise you an exogamous marriage."

Of course you may be one of those people who value intellectual rigor, honesty, friendship, and a fair fight above conversational victory. I think this is a mistake. I know, however, from my anthropological background that it takes all kinds (the first principle of comparative ethnography). If you feel besieged by unscrupulous tribe mentioners, there are ways to defend yourself.

First, pay close attention to the way the tribe is described. If, in the course of a discussion on, say, the importance of mesquite for that smoky taste, or the role of raspberry vinegar in a good sauce, a professional anthropologist (or chef) were to mention the Jalé by name, and discuss their recipes in detail, you would know, at least, that you had a real primitive people to deal with. This is a rare occurrence. Most of the people who talk so much about these tribes aren't anthropologists at all, and they often don't know what tribe they're talking about. They begin with a long, erudite sigh and a sly look, and then they drop it on you. "There's this tribe . . ."

Don't you believe it. Ask who this tribe is, and if the name isn't forthcoming, express grave doubt as to its existence. I know this seems harsh, but people are always mentioning tribes they think their professors mentioned fifteen years ago, but which, in fact, are no more real than the Gazonga, which I must admit I made up. The Gururumba, on the other hand, are real, which proves that truth is more sonorous than fiction. I'm not the only one to make tribes up. Ludwig Wittgenstein, the philosopher, also did so, but he was honest. He would write, for example, "Imagine that the people of a tribe were brought up from early youth to give no expression of feeling *of any kind*." (Then, presumably, they would *never* use italics.)

Something else to look for in tribe aficionados is a slightly tarnished version of the myth of the noble savage. The tribes are, for many of us, the human equivalent of herbal shampoo. People who live in the woods and don't have designer clothes, or even clothes, are assumed to be natural, and therefore better. This isn't necessarily true. Consider the mode of dress of the Jalé. True enough, penis sheaths are morally superior to Jordache jeans and pinky rings. But Jalé men also wear piles of hoops around their waists, which is ridiculous. Furthermore, for every good tribe, there's a bad one. If someone is trying to tell you how much better, more wholesome, and *real* tribal life is, as opposed to the cocaine-ridden treadmills of the better neighborhoods in the Free World, remind him of the Yanomamö. Not only are they devoted to war, but their favorite nonviolent recreation is to spend the afternoon sitting around the rain forest blowing green hallucinogenic dust up their noses.

You needn't counter with a tribe of your own, if you're at a momentary loss for anthropological words. And even if the tribe in question is real, you aren't yet lost. How do we know that the tribe was telling the truth when they told the anthropologist that Coyote stole the secret recipe for boiled maize so the people wouldn't starve when the pine nuts failed? I wouldn't bring up the possibility of mendacity among primitive peoples if it weren't for the recent Margaret Mead brouhaha. You may recall that Margaret Mead came back from Samoa with the news that teenage girls there got to sleep around before they were married and their daddies didn't take their T-birds away. Then, a few years ago, Derek Freeman said this wasn't true, that the parents would never have let them go out riding with boys in the first place, even if they had cars. He said that Mead's informants probably told her fibs to tease her, a form of behavior called by the Samoans *tau fa'ase'e,* or "giving her the business" (my translation). I don't know who's right in this argument. But it does give one pause. If these tribes lied to Margaret Mead, they'd lie to anybody. It may even be that making up stuff to tell anthropologists is the main entertainment of primitive peoples:

First Jalé man: Let's tell him we eat people.

Second Jalé man: Great. And I'll get a bunch of those hoops . . .

If all else fails and one is faced with a real, unarguably extant and truthful tribe, there is a final counterargument, which relies on brutal logic. I'm telling this out of pure altruism, since my wife reads these columns and I'll never again be able to use a tribe to argue her out of a position on what's psychologically healthy. Let's say the argument from the tribe side is that this tribe breast-feeds forever and they're O.K. The counterargument is "Who says they're O.K.?" As professional anthropologists know, just because somebody, somewhere, does something doesn't mean it's good. This point was made most succinctly by a friend's psychoanalyst. My friend had just finished talking about some tribe, probably trying to say that if they didn't need to pay $80 an hour to get along, maybe he didn't either. But were they getting along? "What do we know about these tribes?" the psychiatrist said. "They've never been analyzed." Then, I suppose, he handed over that month's bill.

The Man with No Endorphins

A neurochemical vignette: There's a man, running in the rain, wearing loafers, in Baltimore—it's me. I'm not happy. I'm late for a talk on opiate receptors in the brain because I've been in traffic, then in the new Baltimore subway (which I must say works a lot better than my central nervous system), and finally in the rain, risking life and limb and ruining my shoes. I desperately want to learn more about endorphins and enkephalins, the brain's own opiates, which are supposed to ease pain and produce pleasure, but I know I'm going to be late, and probably wet. (I can never remember: Do you stay drier going faster, or standing very straight under the umbrella and taking tiny steps?) My heart is pounding, my anxiety rising, and my toes are damp. One thought is foremost in my mind. I'm thinking: "Where are my endorphins when I need them?"

I've always been fond of neurochemistry; a field that brings you the opiates of the brain is hard not to like. But neurochemistry hasn't treated me well. I'm sure some brains manufacture these great chemicals, and that the people who have these brains experience runner's high and other pleasant effects. But as near as I can tell my brain doesn't *do* endorphins. When I run I get shin splints and twisted ankles. The most I've ever gotten out of running, in emotional terms, was a momentary absence of anxiety, which I attributed to complete physical exhaustion. It was O.K., but it wasn't that different from being depressed. Runners tell me I never ran far enough. But I happen to know that earthworms have endorphins. Earthworms don't jog. And if invertebrates don't have to run to be happy, I don't see why a higher (or at least taller) vertebrate like myself should have to.

The truth is I'm not even interested in getting high. I'm not greedy. I was happy enough with the mild depression that followed running in the park to continue jogging for years. I stopped only because my twisted ankles refused to heal. What I'm really looking for is absence of pain, a certain kind of pain, which I'll try to define. There is traditional physical pain: cuts and bruises, having your head chopped off. I'm not talking about that. There is traditional psychological pain: Oedipus and Electra complexes, schizophrenia, anxiety neuroses. I'm not talking about that. I'm talking about another class of pain, which occurs in huge quantities every day in my neighborhood. This kind of pain is caused by computers, customer service personnel at banks, medical insurance and expense account forms, and airline baggage personnel, not to mention airlines. Let's call it First World pain.

I know that good people, when their taxes are due or their computers fail, realize that there are people in the world who have schistosomiasis, so that it would be incredibly selfish and insensitive to whine about capital gains or the loss of a great sentence when they still get to eat an unconscionably large amount of protein at dinner, which they don't have to share with blood flukes. Unfortunately, a lot of us aren't good people. A lot of us are bad. A lot of us are so wrapped up in our own little First World lives that taxes and computer failure seem, to us, to cause intense pain, to us.

Out of this sort of selfishness—I myself pay taxes, and have recently experienced computer failure which induced in me not only extreme pain, but guilt for not curing, or having, schistosomiasis—I went to Baltimore to the talk on brain chemicals. Other reporters, I'm sure, were at the conference to report to the public news that would affect their health and welfare, to educate them. I went because I thought I might learn how to find and use my own endorphins. No such luck. Most of the news was about pain messengers—not the people who bring bills and rejection slips in the mail, but peptides that relay the news of tissue damage to the nerve endings so they can send the news to the brain and the brain can cause the mouth of the person with the tissue damage (i.e., a finger that has had the door of a Coupe de Ville slammed shut on it) to howl in pain and indignation. The first messenger in this system is called bradykinin. Bradykinin, according to Solomon Snyder of Johns Hopkins, whose talk I was late for, is the strongest pain-causing substance there is. Fortunately, bradykinin antagonists have been developed to bind the bradykinin before it gets to the nerve endings. Since bradykinin apparently carries messages about arthritis as well as bruised fingers, the antagonist could be rubbed on an arthritic knee (this is all speculative) like old-time liniment, and it would scarf up all the bradykinin and stop the pain. What this could mean to millions of pain sufferers is obvious. What it means to me is that, in neurochemistry, sometimes it does make sense to kill the messenger.

However, to get back to my own pain, which, sad to say, is the subject of greatest interest to me, I have figured out why the endorphins don't work on it. The reason is that human beings were not designed, by evolution, to fill out tax forms, use computers, or fly on commercial airplanes. Now, we weren't designed to play the violin either, as I keep telling a friend of mine when he hauls out his fiddle and starts talking about Paganini.* But when it comes to fiddling we do have what biologists call a pre-adaptation: fingers. They didn't evolve for fiddling; they evolved, as we all know, to play the guitar. But if you've got good ones, they can be used to do hot licks on a Guarneri as well as a Gibson. There is, however, no similar pre-adaptation for dealing with the IRS or airline baggage personnel.

Skeptics among you may be mumbling that there's this tribe that's known for its incredible patience in hunting the dik-dik, but the dik-dik is a more appealing quarry than an old Samsonite suitcase, and the rain forest is preferable to the baggage carousel, even during fever season. In airports, not only do proselytizers try to convert you to obscure religions (opiates, opiates everywhere) but there are crowds of other people whose endorphins are also failing them, and who, for all you know, are about to pull Uzi submachine guns from under their coats and relieve their own pain by causing you to have some. Faced with this situation, the brain is at a loss. It doesn't recognize the pain you're undergoing as something endorphins can take care of, so it lets them sleep and leaves you to fend for yourself, unopiated.

It can be done, assuming, of course, that sooner or later the luggage stumbles through those flaps and the "There's-my-suitcase" neuron lights up. Sometimes that doesn't happen. And now we come to the airline personnel. At an earlier point in my life, when I was in the process of trying to summon up my endorphins, or at least distract myself, by crude means like exercise, I also tried breathing. To be precise, I tried Lamaze, not while giving birth, but in stressful situations. It didn't work, but it did provide me with a

---

*Paganini, on the other hand—on both hands in fact—had long spidery fingers, perhaps because of a genetic aberration called Marfan's syndrome. He *was* designed to play the violin.

tale whose moral is this: Ask not what your endorphins can do for you, but take your fly rod on the airplane with you.

One day a few months before the birth of our second child I was having a fit about some frustrating aspect of home improvement. My wife suggested to me that if Lamaze could get a woman through childbirth, maybe it could get a man through a conversation with an electrician. I tried it. I was never able to find the electrician, and the work is still not done, but I did use controlled breathing to call an airline and get information on flights to Great Falls, Montana. I stayed on the telephone, and kept my voice down for the whole twenty minutes, without benefit of medication.

I then went to Great Falls, Montana, with my wife, niece, first child, incipient second child, and, last but (I'm ashamed to say) not least, my prized fly rod. We were going to hike, fish, and look at dinosaur bones. You know what happened. I checked the fly rod and the airline lost it. I stood at the baggage counter, breathing—in, out, in, out, managing the pain—and filled out a form. (Have I emphasized forms as a source of pain?) We went to the hotel, and four days later I was told, in a telephone conversation (my wife was next to me with a cup of cracked ice, coaching me on my breathing), that the rod had been retrieved from Angola and sent to Kalispell, Montana, on the other side of the continental divide from the Many Glacier Hotel, to which I had been sent. The man from the airline, in the single most infuriating conversation I've ever had, replied to my calm, reasoned statement that I wasn't in Kalispell by telling me that that's where I should have been. There were more frequent flights to that airport, and, he said to me, as I stood there rodless and dumbfounded, the fishing was better over there.

I wasn't arrested for what I said into the telephone, but I could have been. Frankly, I don't see why, if these endorphins are going to be so fickle, we can't have more doctors around. When you're all worked up, there's nothing like general anaesthesia. I did eventually get the fly rod back, just as we were about to leave to go dig dinosaurs, and I used it a few more times that summer, back East. Optimists will see in this resolution a benevolent, smiling universe. Realists will see that the paragraph isn't over yet. On my last day of fishing (I didn't know it was my last day of fishing), I put the fly rod on the top of the car and, due to some faulty synapses, drove off. I heard a rattle, and in the side mirror I saw my rod leap into the air, do a barrel roll, and dive under the wheels of a pickup truck. There was nothing left but splinters. My endorphins, as usual, were nowhere to be seen.

A Serf in the Kingdom of Vegetables

*And God said ... let them have dominion over the fish of
the sea, and over the fowl of the air, and over the cattle, and
over all the earth, and over every creeping thing that creepeth
upon the earth.*

—Genesis 1:26

G od didn't mention Japanese knotweed. Oh, there's
that bit of hand waving about "all the earth" and
some later references to herbs and fruits. But it
seems to me that He left the question of where we stand in
relation to plants somewhat vague. God was no dummy.

I used to like plants. But that was when I lived in an
apartment. To me, a plant was a little green thing in an
orange pot that needed to be watered, misted, and protected
from mites. Plants were light, pleasant, undemanding, like
salad, except they were still dirty. Then I moved to a house,
a house that came with an overgrown plot of land that I
saw, in a burst of romantic vision, as a yard. I discovered
that plants in the wild are to house plants as the rats on
the banks of the Ganges are to gerbils. The things that
grew in my yard didn't need my protection; they didn't need
anybody's protection. This is what a writer in *Horticulture*

magazine wrote about the things that grew in my yard—
"Viciously aggressive, rampant, and perniciously invasive,
these plants are best avoided."

I now believe that most outdoor plants are pernicious,
but the writer was describing two particular species, one
of which covered a good quarter-acre in my yard (the rest
was sumac, brambles, wild cherry, and poison ivy). That
plant is known, in the vernacular, as bamboo, Japanese
knotweed, Mexican bamboo, or "He That Eateth Up the
Yards of the Unjust."* It isn't real bamboo, however, but
either a member of the smartweed family, an apt name, or
closely related. Scientifically it's called *Polygonum cuspidatum* or *Reynoutria japonica*. I believe that plants are like
people in that if they have a lot of aliases, you should watch
out for them.

I once called the plant hotline of the New York Botanical
Garden in the Bronx—which is like poison control for lawns.
When I told them what plant I was fighting, the person on
the other end laughed. The same thing happens if you tell
a poison control volunteer you've just swallowed cyanide.
And for the same reason—it's an attempt to stave off black
despair with humor. I'm sure it seems silly that someone
could go on like this about a plant. But it isn't. I quote from
Weed Control in the Home Garden, a pamphlet published
by the Brooklyn Botanic Garden: "There are no sure-fire
cultural practices that will control Japanese knotweed.
Covering an infested area with two inches of asphalt in a
driveway is futile, as the new shoots push right through
the asphalt. Several layers of black polyethylene film tightly
applied to a leveled soil surface and covered with asphalt,
patio blocks, or stones may be an answer (but at considerable price for the average homeowner)."

You realize that the writer of that paragraph said that

---

*Maybe the just too. I can't speak for them.

if I spread polyethylene over a quarter of an acre and then pave it, that *may* be an answer.

In botanical terms Japanese knotweed is an "escaped ornamental." It's native to Japan, and according to one account was taken to England by a Belgian in 1864. It came to the U.S. in the late nineteenth century along with a relative from the island of Sakhalin known as giant knotweed, which is much the same, only bigger. Somehow, sometime, the thing got out of a garden or escaped from a hillside it had been meant to hold from erosion and made its way, over hill and dale, to my yard, which it's in the process of consuming. In his classic *Weeds,* the late Walter Conrad Muenscher, who was given to understatement, said that Japanese knotweed was "spreading rapidly and becoming obnoxious." Muenscher was too kind. I think it always was obnoxious.

For instance, cutting only prompts more growth, so that haphazard slashing results in more, not less, bamboo. And the thing has huge food storage capacities underground, probably in preparation for a nuclear attack, which I've considered.* Before I knew about its qualities, I chopped and mowed a plot to a grisly stubble one day. In two weeks the bamboo was chin high and laughing. It also sends out runners and rhizomes underground. In my neighborhood, it has leaped paved streets, which has caused one neighbor to hang cloves of garlic on his doors and windows. This is pure superstition because the plant also reproduces by seeds, against which garlic has no effect. A more practical solution is to fly over your yard at dawn in a fleet of gunships, blaring Wagner, and scorch the earth with lethal herbicides. But this isn't the kind of persona one likes to assume, even against weeds.

*A grove of real bamboo (almost as tough as knotweed) at ground zero at Hiroshima survived the blast and sprouted within days.

Besides, if you make a mistake with anything that can kill bamboo, it will do to your yard what God did to Sodom and Gomorrah. And nobody promises that anything will, in fact, kill bamboo. They say it could, or it may. As in "repeated sprayings of the Japanese-bamboo foliage with [dicamba and 2,4-D] could bring it under control" (which is the considered opinion of the authors of *Weed Control in the Home Garden*). As to what 2,4-D *could* do to any laboratory rats (escaped "experimentals") that happened to be hiding out in the bamboo, that's a matter of some dispute. However, a wild-eyed Health, Education, and Welfare advisory committee (no doubt under the demonic influence of Ralph Nader) once recommended that the herbicide be banned. With chemicals, there's always the chance of laying waste to the entire yard, or neighborhood, and leaving only the bamboo still alive.

As bad as it is, bamboo alone wasn't able to turn me against the whole vegetable kingdom. It took the rest of my yard to do that. It started with the locusts. (I don't mean the insects, for which I now feel a good deal of affection, but trees, which are members of the legume family.) The seed pods of honey locusts are good to eat. But the seeds, roots, bark, and leaves of black locusts are poisonous. (My guidebooks disagree about the flowers.) It isn't so easy to tell a black locust from a honey locust. I can't even tell them apart when I look at the pictures in the guidebook, and when I try counting leaves in the "wild" I'm lost. The only way I can figure to find out what kind of trees I've got is to eat a few pods, which I'm sure is just what the locusts have in mind.

I also have mulberries, gentle, friendly, fruit-bearing trees, I thought. But the unripe mulberries contain hallucinogens. I'm past the age at which I'm willing to gather and smoke unripe mulberries, nor do I want my yard filled with people who are willing. But that's the least of my problems. I also have horse chestnuts, pokeweed, and ivy, all poisonous in one part or another. I have rhubarb, the leaves of which contain oxalic acid. And around the house are planted yew trees, mountain laurel, rhododendrons, and azaleas, all bad. As one of my field guides says of the rhododendron family: "The ornamental bushes surrounding our houses may be deadly strangers waiting to kill the unwary . . . many of these plants possess a deadly poison that was used by the Delaware Indians as a suicide potion."

Nice shrubs. They have a clever little adromedotoxin that stimulates heart nerves and then blocks them, "leading to death by heart failure." Even the good parts of my yard are death traps. If capital punishment ever becomes widespread again they could bring condemned felons out here for a day in the country. Instead of the electric chair they could do a wild-foods lunch. "Here, Humongus, try a little of this rhododendron salad. Some pokeweed? Mountain laurel tea?"

I've even read of plants communicating, by chemicals, about the attacks of predators, so that they can all get the poisons out there in the leaf tips before the bugs start chewing. Not only did I have deadly strangers for foundation plantings, but they were also talking behind my back.

When I realized that this—the bamboo (which, to its credit, is edible) attacking my yard, and my bushes attacking me—was the famed community of life that environmentalists and evolutionists were always going on about, and over which I myself had occasionally gotten misty-eyed, I threw out my Darwin and started reading *Weed Control in the Home Garden* and the Old Testament. The first gave me technique, the second moral support. I reread Genesis to find out what God had to say about homeowners having dominion over their yards. What He said unto them (Adam and Eve in my reading) finally explained to me what had happened to my yard. After Adam and Eve ate the apple, God invented weeds. Before the fact, He said, "Replenish the earth, and subdue it" (easy for Him to say). After, He said, "Thorns also and thistles shall it bring forth to thee." I interpret the Bible liberally and take the thorns and thistles to include *Polygonum cuspidatum*. He also predicted how hard it would be to get the thorns and thistles out of your yard, saying "In the sweat of thy face shalt thou eat bread." I suspect this is the origin of the expression "In your face!"

I saw the light. I shed my evolutionist plant sympathies. I began to look on mowing the lawn as a Biblical struggle. When I got out the old rotary mower and filled it with gasoline, I thought to myself, "Subdue the earth," or, for variety's sake, "Smite the Hittites." I even hired a young man who smote a lot harder than I did. He did to my yard what Joshua was wont to do to the lands of his enemies. He "smote all the country of the hills, and of the south, and of the vale, and of the springs . . . he left none remaining."

Except the bamboo. I wouldn't say it's still standing, it's more like kneeling, or sneaking around in runners and rhizomes. And it has been forced to share the ground with grass. But it's far from dead. This spring I may resort to chemicals, perhaps even Wagner. But I'm not sure. Rumor has it that one man in town, driven bamboo-mad, assaulted the stuff with a chemical so bad that it's legal only in Texas. There's fear in the community now for future generations. But the fear is only in the human population. His bamboo is doing fine.

The Sociobiology of
Humor in Cats
and Dogs

There are times in life when you have to speak up. People may heap calumny or contumely on you, depending on their vocabulary. They may even ignore you. But you can't ignore the call of conscience. I'm talking about the kind of moral imperative that made Rachel Carson write *Silent Spring* and the Kingston Trio sing about Charlie on "The MTA." Not that I put myself in the same moral class as the Kingston Trio, but I too have a message that I feel compelled to deliver, whatever the consequences: dogs are better than cats.

I don't mean that I like dogs better than cats. Nor do I mean that dogs are better for certain things, like feet warming, while cats are better for other things, like appearing in fashion advertisements. I'm not saying that dogs are better looking than cats, or smarter, or that they have more cartoons drawn of them. They're certainly not cleaner. However, dogs have a sense of humor. Cats don't. And I can prove it. That sense of humor is what makes dogs better—purely, absolutely, ontologically better.

The only reason I bring this up is that I think cats are causing the decline of civilization. Two prime examples of their effect on modern life are the disappearance of literacy and the appalling condition of modern bookstores, both directly attributable not to MTV but to cat books and calendars. If you look at these things you'll see that they're full of pictures and cartoons. Dog books have words. Think of what dogs have done for literature: *Lad: A Dog* and *The Call of the Wild,* the tales and cartoons of Thurber, even Snoopy, who, although a cartoon character, appears in a strip in which the name Beethoven is occasionally mentioned. Ranged against these we have Garfield and his sort, who monopolize all the good spots near the cash register. What would Shakespeare say?

I also blame cats for the rise of narcissism. Cats are the ultimate narcissists. You can tell this because of all the time they spend on personal grooming. Dogs aren't like this. A dog's idea of personal grooming is to roll in a dead fish. Dogs spend their time thinking about doing good deeds for their masters, or sleeping.

Implicit in my criticism of cats is what might be called the "petogenic" theory of culture. We've known for a long time that individual persons tend to resemble their pets. I think the same is true of societies. Do we want to become a nation of Morrises? Is America to be nothing more than a picky eater? Even physiologically cats are finicky; they're obligate carnivores, or strict meat-eaters. Dogs, on the other hand (or mouth), are omnivores in the true sense of the word. Waste not, want not is the motto of all dogs. They live in a permanent Third World of the mind where the notion of throwing out food is incomprehensible. Let even a King Charles spaniel off its leash and it will head straight for the neighbor's garbage can, where it will consume anything that's edible, or has been next to something edible, and spread the rest around the street. I think this is done for moral and comic purposes, as well as those of appetite. While cats are lying on divans waiting for the next flavor surprise, dogs are reproaching us for throwing out perfectly good gristle.

I didn't make this up about dogs having a sense of humor. Well, actually I did make it up. Then I found that some famous dead scientists agreed with me, like Charles Darwin. In *The Descent of Man* he said, "Dogs show what may be fairly called a sense of humour." In this opinion he was supported by George Romanes, another great man of science, also dead, in whose work I found the Darwin quotation. Romanes was one of the founders of the study of animal behavior and he credited dogs, but not cats, with "the emotion of the ludicrous."

What Romanes did credit the cat with was "disadvantages of temperament." I think he meant that cats aren't nice. There are those who say that when cats torture crippled mice (which they themselves have crippled) they're not enjoying themselves. You might as well say that William F. Buckley Jr. doesn't enjoy winning arguments. As Romanes says, "The feelings that prompt a cat to torture a captured mouse can only, I think, be assigned to the category to which by common consent they are ascribed—delight in torturing for torture's sake." Needless to say, neither Romanes nor I believe that laughing at a crippled mouse counts as having a sense of humor.

In contrast, Romanes said that dogs had the ability both to tell and appreciate a good joke. As one bit of evidence he discussed his own terrier, which "used, when in good humour, to perform several tricks, which I know to have been self-taught, and which clearly had the object of exciting laughter. For instance, while lying on his side and violently grinning, he would hold one leg in his mouth." So much for the intelligence of dogs. But I never said they were smart. And as jokes go, this isn't a bad one. Surely you've seen more than one comedian who would have been more amusing if he had put his leg in his mouth and grinned.

The usual criticism of Romanes is that he was guilty of

anthropomorphism. But as far as I'm concerned, animals *are* like people, and I believe science is coming around to this point of view. Consider the talking apes, the chimpanzees Washoe, Lana, and Nim, and the gorilla Koko. Not only does Koko have language, or something like it, but she also had a pet—a pet kitten. If having a pet doesn't make you like a human being, I don't know what does. (Too bad it was a kitten.) Furthermore, Donald Griffin at Rockefeller University has made persuasive arguments for animals having consciousness, at least when they're awake. And at the extreme left on the anthropomorphism issue, the animal rights movement claims for animals the same rights that human beings enjoy. The message of this movement is not that animals are *like* people but that they *are* people.

This new, and welcome, anthropomorphism doesn't quite prove Romanes's argument, however, and I did promise proof. For that we need sociobiology. If you recall, sociobiology is the scientific discipline in which you pick a behavior, like being rich, and construct a good story of how it evolved to show that it's genetic, and not the result of trust funds. (Critics sometimes claim that sociobiologists miss the subtle distinction between "inheritance" and "heredity.") If I tried this approach with my argument, I'd be in trouble. I can't start with my conclusion—dog humor—and then construct a story. That would be begging the question. So I'll start with the story. If it's good enough, I'm sure we'll agree that the behavior must exist.

This is my story:

Once upon a time, the ancestors of dogs—wolves in layman's language—found the stresses and strains of life in a hierarchical social species unbearable. They lived in packs dominated by alpha (not Alpo) males who pushed around all the other males. Everybody knew everybody else's business. Nobody had any privacy. And on top of that they mated for life. Consequently, they did the only thing possible: they developed a sense of humor.

How this worked in terms of evolutionary genetics is that the dog ancestors that had no sense of humor didn't live long enough to produce offspring. Put yourself in the proto-dog's position. Let's say you're a young male wolf without a mate. The rest of the males are always coming out of the den in the morning with big grins on their faces. By the time you get your turn at the moose carcass, all that's left are the chewy parts. You can't laugh it off, because you're genetically incapable of humor, so you lose control and attack the alpha wolf. He kills you. You know what that means—no offspring for you. Natural selection has just eliminated your no-sense-of-humor genes from the wolf gene pool.

It has, by the way, been scientifically demonstrated that wolves have a lot to laugh off. In a study of the wolves on Isle Royale, Michigan, in Lake Superior, the wolves succeeded in killing the moose only six times in 131 moose hunts. If these wolves were a football team they would be the New Orleans Saints. With ancestors like that, you end up appreciating the absurdity of life, not to mention moose hunts. And when you (a dog descendant) are faced with a human owner wielding a rolled-up newspaper, pointing to the rug, and shouting "Did you do that?" you do what your ancestors did when they missed the moose. You stuff your leg in your mouth and grin.

Cats are different. Cats have pride and dignity. Animals that live in hierarchical social systems (people, for instance) can afford pride and dignity only if they're at the top of the ladder. If you're a cat, you *are* the ladder. Put yourself in the proto-cat's place. Odds are you're a solitary carnivore. You live alone. Once in a great while you mate with a stranger who also has claws. On an average day you get up, kill something, eat it, and go back to sleep. What's funny? Laughing has no evolutionary benefits, and consequently you have no sense of humor. This is the evolutionary history of domestic cats. This is why cats are remote, independent, and mean. They don't tell jokes, and when you tell one, they don't laugh.

In other words, dogs are better (Q.E.D.). And they're more suited to us as a species. If you "miss the moose" at work a dog can sympathize with your plight. If you like, you can even blame the dog. It's genetically prepared to take this in good humor, and it will urge you to do the same when unjust accusations are leveled at you. In the same situation a cat will scorn you for being weak, and point out that when it feels bad, it kills something. I don't think this attitude is helpful. In fact, I firmly believe that as a people (or perhaps I should say "as people") we're less likely to cause a nuclear war if we keep dogs, not cats, as pets.

One final note: I know that emotions run high on this issue. It's conceivable that I might have offended some cat lovers, and that they might want to send me insulting letters, to which I would have to invent clever replies. To save them and me a lot of time and trouble, I thought I'd print the reply I have ready for them right now. It's a quotation from Romanes. After describing the cruelty of cats he said something that I like so much I'm adopting it as a response to all letters about this piece, perhaps to all letters about anything: "With regard to cats it is needless to dwell further upon facts so universally known."

Royal Flush: Travels in the Toilet Trade

I suppose the first order of business is to explain why I'm writing about toilets. I'm not doing it just so I can get in a little bathroom humor. Not that I'm opposed to low comedy, vulgarity, or shameless chasing after laughs. In principle, I'm in favor of all those things. It's just that my primary interest in toilets is in the mechanisms in the tanks, the valves and arms and floats, the things that hiss, roar, and gurgle, the stuff that is to the overall toilet what a central processing unit is to a computer. Call it toilet science.

I'm not claiming that it takes quantum theory or recombinant DNA to develop a good toilet, although it does take good toilets to develop quantum theory. (The modern theoretical physicist depends on indoor plumbing.) Inventing and perfecting toilet mechanisms does, however, depend on a knowledge of mechanical engineering. You need to understand water pressure and valves, too. I suppose that as an intellectual adventure, making a toilet tank valve may not compare to inventing general relativity or finding a cure for cancer. But if you consider the contribution of plumbing to human life, the other sciences fade into insignificance. Good toilets have done more for public health than all the doctors since Hippocrates. In fact, toilets are one of the few

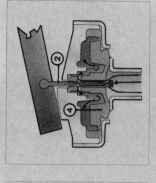

FLUIDMASTER

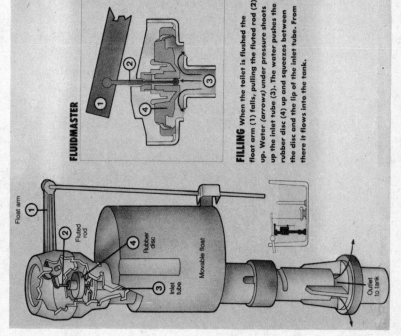

Float arm ①

② Fluted rod

④ Rubber disc

③ Inlet tube

Movable float

Outlet to tank

FILLING When the toilet is flushed the float arm (1) falls, pulling the fluted rod (2) up. Water (arrows) under pressure shoots up the inlet tube (3). The water pushes the rubber disc (4) up and squeezes between the disc and the lip of the inlet tube. From there it flows into the tank.

FILLED As the tank fills, the float rises and the fluted rod (2) drops. Now the hole in the rubber disc (4) is open, allowing water to flow under pressure into the space above the disc. The water pushes the disc down, sealing the inlet tube and stopping the flow of water into the tank.

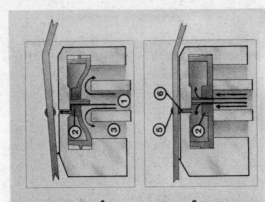

FILLPRO

Rubber pad · Hole · Rubber disc · Diaphragm

Baffles

Inlet tube

Outlet to tank

FILLING When the toilet is flushed, water *(arrows)* surges up the inlet tube (1). A small amount squirts through a hole in a rubber disc (2). The rest is deflected down by the disc through a system of baffles (3) and into the toilet tank.

FILLED As the tank fills, water pushes down on the diaphragm (4, in the large drawing). A rubber pad (5) on the diaphragm's arm seals a hole (6). This traps water above the disc (2), forcing it down against the inlet tube, and sealing the tube off.

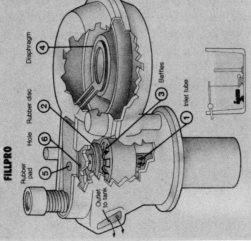

Joe Le Monnier © DISCOVER MAGAZINE 5/86

purely benevolent technological objects. Physicists may have known sin when they invented the bomb, but the worst thing the people who design toilet machinery are guilty of is a fondness for bad jokes.*

What attracted me to toilet technology is that it seemed comprehensible in a way that most of the world is not. I do not, in any fundamental way, understand my computer, my tape deck, or the telephone. I know that if I push the right numbers on the telephone I'll get my editor, or an ear-piercing whine that I figure is AT&T's revenge for being dismantled; that if I tap the right keys on my computer, this sentence will appear on the screen; that if I push the "play" button on my tape deck Johnny Cash will sing "I've been flushed from the bathroom of your heart."† But don't ask me why.

Toilets are different. The principle is simple. Water fills a tank. You flush. Some kind of valve lets enough water back in to fill the tank. In the old ballcock system, a float ball at the end of a metal arm rises with the water level, forcing down a stopper of some kind at the other end of the arm. Ballcocks are comprehensible, but lacking in romance. However, while all the science and technology buffs have been tinkering with computers, a world of toilet machinery has appeared. These mechanisms started to come out in the 1960s and '70s, and now they've taken over the hardware stores. They're plastic. They don't have long arms and float

---

*One company gives away ceramic coffee mugs shaped like toilet bowls, each graced with the legend "Think Tank." Obviously people in the toilet business have a sense of humor, although, given their sense of humor, it's a good thing they're in the toilet business.

†This song, by Jack Clement, also has lines like, "in the garbage disposal of your mind, I've been ground up dear." It's proof that C. P. Snow was wrong when he lamented the separation of the arts and the sciences in his famous essay "The Two Cultures." Look what happened when music (an art) met plumbing (a science). I plan to refute Snow soon in my own essay, entitled "Two Cultures Are Better Than None."

balls. Their inner workings are hidden. And yet they shut off water flow quickly, without that drawn-out hiss the ball-cocks are so good at. The new gadgets have the mystery of high technology, but they're simple enough to be understood completely, from flush to full.

Or so I told myself. The new mechanisms presented a challenge—to go where no science writer had gone before, into the toilet tank, and to penetrate what the 1611 charter of England's Worshipful Company of Plumbers called "the art and the mystery." I accepted the challenge.

I'd found in the course of my research that California was a hotbed of toilet tank valve development and production. Fluidmaster, the McDonald's of the business, in one competitor's words, was near Los Angeles, in Anaheim. Fillpro was two hours south in Carlsbad, just north of San Diego. Fillpro makes a valve like no other I've seen. It has no float at all and looks like nothing so much as a tiny, covered frying pan. Two small companies, both engaged in the search for the perfect flush, in California—it added up to only one thing: Toilet Valley. I flew to the Coast.

On the airplane I read a British history of bathrooms called *Clean and Decent* by Lawrence Wright. I recommend it highly. It's worth reading for the headings alone, among my favorites being "No Soap for Bacon," "Clean Queens," and "The Dauphin Commits a Nuisance." The book notes that the Minoans were among the first to have good plumbing. In the palace at Knossos they had terrific toilets with wooden seats, some of which may have had flushing mechanisms. The ancient Egyptians equipped their privies with stone seats. (It's a good thing they didn't live in Vermont.) Anyone interested in writing an unscrupulous best-seller, or headlines for the *National Enquirer* (and there are more of us than you might think), cannot help but notice that the pharaohs sat on these toilet seats. Since the pharaohs were supposedly divine, it would be safe to call these old stone potties the "Toilets of the Gods."

The toilets of the rest of us began to get fancy in 1596, when the first valve closet was invented, although it wasn't until the late 1700s that others like it came into use. Flushing toilets, as we know them, began to appear in the late 1800s. Several kinds were invented. *Clean and Decent* doesn't even mention Thomas Crapper, who I had been led to believe was the father of the flush toilet. Apparently he was just one of its many uncles.

From a contemplation of this long and distinguished past, I stepped off my plane into what I assumed was the toilet future—Los Angeles. At 3 A.M. my time, before I went to sleep in a vast bed that the Holiday Inn had draped with the finest petro-fiber blankets, I tried, like any good journalist would, to get the top off the toilet tank. I was unsuccessful. It was screwed down tight with one large Phillips head screw. By some inexplicable oversight I had neglected to bring a Phillips head screwdriver with me. Whatever the secret of Holiday Inn toilets is, it's safe. I wonder, do people steal toilet tank fill valves from motels?

The next morning, on my way to Fluidmaster, I made another research stop at Disneyland. Mickey was there, Pluto, Snow White, and some dwarfs. I saw Fantasyland and Frontierland. The park doesn't have a Toiletland, per se, but it does have toilets. From my point of view, however, they were disappointing. Disneyland toilets, at least the ones I used, don't have individual tanks with fill valves in them. I took my Mickey Mouse and Goofy dolls and headed up State College Boulevard to Via Burton.

Fluidmaster is on Via Burton. Fluidmaster is to toilet tank fill valves what Sony is to Walkmen. It makes something like six million fill valves a year. While I was touring Fluidmaster, it quickly became clear that plumbing science was different from other kinds of science. For one thing there was the decor. On the wall of one office at Fluidmaster was a calendar with a photograph of a lovely woman in a red bikini posed by the sea with a Ridgid Model 2A Pipe-cutter. If I remember right, her name was Lois. On a more technical level, it was a treat to stand in Fluidmaster's highly automated factory under an overhead conveyor belt that was carrying, slowly, 40,000 new toilet tank fill valves. It would be futile to seek a metaphor to explain what it is like to have 40,000 toilet tank fill valves pass overhead. I leave it to the imagination.

The valve itself turned out to be one of those things, like marriage, that are simple in principle but complicated in practice (see diagram on page 71). And, after all, why shouldn't it be? Why should something that saves so many people from typhoid and toilet hiss be easy to understand? I say this after having had a Fluidmaster executive talk me through a flush cycle, just the way Sky King used to talk down those twelve-year-olds in Piper Cubs. I crashed.

At first, that is; at first all I could see were the parts—the channel through which water flowed, rubber discs, a pencil-thin, fluted metal rod (controlled by a float), which moved through the rubber discs, opening them or sealing them off, and other stuff. The principle involved, I was told, was that of turning water against itself. Once the tank was full, the water was forced into a place where it pressed down on one of the discs and sealed the whole thing off. I failed to see how any of this occurred.

In fact, as we got deeper and deeper into the Fluidmaster mechanism, the purpose of the fluting on the rod, and the flexing of the discs, I felt myself slipping away. I didn't actually lose consciousness, although I was tempted. I didn't manage to stay fully awake, either. At the moment of deep-est puzzlement I had a waking dream of the kind that has been known to crystallize other great insights. It came to me that what I was looking at wasn't a mechanism, but a little boy in funny clothes . . . from Europe perhaps . . . maybe Alsace-Lorraine. Then I saw the wooden shoes. The kid wasn't Alsatian at all. He was from the Netherlands! Fluidmaster had created, out of rubber and metal, a little Dutch boy who would reliably stick his finger in the right place at the right time, and do for your bathroom and mine what the original did for Holland.

I don't want to seem too smug about this. But I must say that having understood how so complex and important a piece of technology worked, I did feel a surge of renewed confidence, a certain legitimacy about living in the modern world, and a tremendous sense of relief. I was certain there was an aura of knowledge and power surrounding me as I drove down the Pacific Coast Highway, although that may have emanated not from me but from the brand-new flamingo red Camaro the rental car company had forced me to accept in lieu of my usual writerly sedan.

The next morning, after I stayed at an inn with a run-on toilet (which I fixed handily), I continued on to Fillpro, which is in Carlsbad in a new corporate park. It didn't look like a plumbing company. It had tinted windows and a color coordinated waiting room, which made me suspicious. Was Fillpro serious about toilets, or was it trying to get into computers? I'm happy to say that, judging from our extended, unbelievably detailed fill valve discussions, the company is very serious about toilets. And its valve is not only an engineering but also an aesthetic triumph (see diagram on page 72), if one can speak in these terms of toilet valves. It has no float, and no fluted rod. It has just one moving part. The whole thing sticks up only about three inches from the bottom of the tank. It too forces water to work against itself, but it does it *invisibly*.

I'm not going to tell you exactly how it works. It's a cardinal principle of science writing never to make your readers lose consciousness. But I'll give you a hint. The moving part may look like a frying pan, but it acts like a seesaw. When the pan end of the seesaw is down, that makes the incoming water do exactly what it does in the Fluidmaster set-up—shut itself off. I saw the valve at work in a see-through toilet tank, an object that I covet for my own home. I watched it flush and fill. No motion was visible in the Fillpro valve. It remained serene as the water rushed out and the water rushed in. Then all was quiet.

I don't yet have a transparent toilet tank in my home. I do have a Fillpro in one toilet, a Fluidmaster in another, and an old ballcock in a third. I think this is what journalistic objectivity is all about. But as inspiring as it was to learn how toilets work, I have to say that it wasn't the high point of my trip. That, as it turned out, had to do with the economic, not the scientific, side of plumbing. When I got to Fillpro and asked if I could use the bathroom, I was refused. The plumbing was out. During my entire tour of the plant the bathrooms were unusable, and plumbers were either searching for the problem or on their break. You can imagine how I felt. The prospect of a plumbing company about to be charged a fortune by plumbers will cause extreme and irresistible glee to toilet owners everywhere. I've nothing against Fillpro, but it's nice to know that while there may not be justice in the world, at least there's irony.

À la Recherche des Crayolas Perdus

F rom the inexhaustible engine of commerce comes now Aromance, the Aroma Disc system. Actually it came a few years ago, but I've been trying to ignore it. It doesn't mind. It sits patiently on the counter at my local Captain Video, daring me to try it. (I guess selling aroma records and videotapes in the same store is the retail equivalent of synaesthesia.) Aroma discs are about the size of small computer floppy discs. You slip them into a box (only $14.95), and as the disc is warmed, a mist or smoke emerges with the scent of Passion, Fireplace, or After Dinner Mints. I've resisted buying an aroma disc machine. The thing frightens me. If an electrical fire is about to burn down the house or someone left the gas on, I don't want Country Moods confusing my smelling apparatus. More important, I don't want to be part of a world in which a man and a woman, on a romantic anniversary, turn to each other and whisper, "Honey, they're playing our smell."

I'm sure people will say this anyway. My buying habits seem to have about the same effect as my vote. And smells are, and have been for a while, a big, strange business. On a mundane level there's Lemon Fresh Joy and pine-scented cleaners. Manufacturers stick "clean" scents in their laundry detergents. Scent-impregnated magazine inserts are now so common that my three-year-old daughter thinks the only purpose of *Vogue* is to bring her perfume. She rubs them on her wrists—Opium and Obsession, which I suppose will be followed by Heroin and Paranoia—and asks me if she smells pretty.

Some enterprising souls are engaged in smell therapy, not helping people smell, or smell better, but using odors to help them feel better. Spiced apple is supposed to calm you down. International Flavors & Fragrances, the Dow Chemical of commercial smells, makes aerosol cans filled with the aromas of pizza, ham, new cars, anything that might entice somebody to buy something they might otherwise not. Society is everywhere losing its odor integrity. A Florida marine museum has sprayed its exhibits with sea smell. A few years ago Monsanto reported that it had synthesized a "fresh air" smell, which, of course, would be a silly thing to do if we actually had fresh air. And about three years ago, in what may be, aesthetically, the odor crime of the century, a company in Ohio came out with a cherry-scented garden hose.

It may seem that I'm some kind of weird odor curmudgeon, looking for something new to complain about now that television is all used up. After all, why not douse everything in a scent? Perfumes have been around forever. Human beings have always covered up one scent with another—as they should, sometimes. The paper diaper companies can perfume their products without criticism from me. I believe everyone who rides the subway should use deodorant. I'm all in favor of Chanel No. 5. But none of these uses of scents is deceptive. I know what's in diapers; I don't need to know what everybody on the subway smells like; and men and women who adorn themselves with perfumes aren't trying to pass as flowers. They just want to please their dancing partners.

It's the fake smells I don't like, the ones that are meant

to fool you. This is a dangerous business, because the human nose is fragile, emotional, and neither very bright nor, usually, very well trained.* Most of us have a poor vocabulary for odors. (The study of odors, however, has wonderful words, like "phantasmia" for an olfactory hallucination, and "olfactorium," the smelling equivalent of soundproof room, also called, in Latin, a *camera inodorata*.) Inside the brain, smell seems closely connected to the centers for emotion and cooking. It's snuggled right up to sex, anger, and blackened redfish. Obviously, the sense of smell is a prime target for manipulation. As perfumers have always known, love may be blind, but it's not anosmic.

Writers as well as perfumers know the power of smell. Marcel Proust set off the connections between smell (or taste, which is inextricably intertwined with smell), emotion, and memory with a crumb of petite madeleine swamped by tea. This doesn't work for me, perhaps because I don't know exactly what a petite madeleine is. But I recently discovered another substance that has roughly the same effect. What I use isn't a little French cake, but it is an object of childhood, as was Proust's madeleine. I stimulate my odor memory with a fresh box of Crayola crayons.

You see why I've yet to write a great French novel. But writers and smellers both have to work with what they have, and in our house we have children and crayons. I don't expect you to experience the Crayola smell just by thinking about crayons, since most people can't recall smells the way they can recall pictures or sounds. I expect you to go out and buy a box. Take it to a quiet (and not too smelly) place, an olfactorium if you've got one, flip open the lid, and

*Perfumers and wine tasters do train their sense of smell. Not long ago there was a man who sniffed fish for the U.S. Food and Drug Administration, and there may still be one. There being no acceptable test for rottenness in fish, for national fish security the government was relying on a human nose.

sniff. I don't mean wave it under your nose as if you were a courtier appreciating a jonquil. Get your nose, big or little, right down on the crayons, and inhale deeply. Pull that crayon smell right up into the old reptile brain. Once you get a good whiff of waxy crayon odor, the bells of childhood will ring. Unless your parents beat you with those little sticks of "red-violet" and "yellow-green," you'll be flooded with a new-crayon, clean-piece-of-paper, untouched-coloring-book feeling—you're young, the world is new, the next thing you know your parents may bring home a puppy.

For a while after I discovered this effect, I did a lot of surreptitious crayon sniffing. Not that I was ashamed of it, but when my kids caught me, they took the crayons away. Children live by rigid social rules, and they know that crayons belong to children as absolutely as bourbon and scissors belong to adults. Up in my office, with the door closed, I would open the plastic bag from Toys "Я" Us (slowly, so it didn't crinkle too loudly), take out my box of 64 colors, and snarf up the crayon vapors. It took me some time, and some outside research, to get the higher levels of my brain involved so that I could see (not smell, you understand, but see) why it was that smelling crayons made me feel good. I finally realized that the smell of crayons isn't just an odor, it's part of our culture, something in the same class as the Howdy Doody song, and with the same resonance. In the future, long after they've stopped drawing with crayons, my daughters will have in their brains, as I do now, the useless and thoroughly inappropriate information that if you smell stearic acid you're about to have a good time.*

---

*That's the major component in the smell of Crayola crayons, according to the Crayola company, officially called Binney & Smith, which makes two billion crayons a year. That means there's at least one Crayola crayon for every family on earth. Not every family gets its crayons, however. In our house alone we've massed the allotments of whole crayonless villages.

If crayons can have that kind of effect, you can see why I'm wary about odor manipulation. Not the perfumes. The world can live with seduction. What I don't want is Ronald Reagan dousing my neighborhood with spiced apple smell to make me think I'm happy. I don't want the planet crop-dusted with "fresh air" smell, so I can't tell what I'm breathing. I don't want the smell of pizza to come out of a machine. I want to keep my nose tuned to reality, so I'll be able to smell a rat, or the blood of an Englishman. And I want everyone else to know it when I raise a stink because there's something fishy going on.

I like crayons because they have odor integrity. The Crayola people didn't stick stearic acid into their product to make you buy it. Nobody in his right mind would buy something because it smelled like a fatty acid. If there were a national odor museum, and there should be one (between the national restaurant and the national wine bar), I would give crayons pride of place in it.

And I would surround them with other objects with honest aromas that make up American odor culture. I have a few ideas of what these other objects should be. I got my ideas from William Cain of Yale and the John B. Pierce Foundation Laboratory in New Haven. Cain, who's also president of the New York Academy of Sciences, is involved in studying many aspects of olfaction. Other people might describe his line of work as the psychology and psychophysics of sensation. He calls it the smell game. As part of one of his experiments he had people sniff eighty everyday things, and he ranked the substances in terms of how recognizable their odors were. His list is the place for the aroma preservationist to begin, being full of things with wonderful and memorable smells.

On it are Juicy Fruit and Vick's Vapo Rub (remember getting it rubbed into your chest?), Ivory soap, baby powder, bleach, and pencil shavings. (Remember grammar school?

Remember driving that freshly sharpened pencil into the top of Billy Donnelly's head and telling him he would die of lead poisoning? Sure you do.) Cain also tested Band-Aids, nail polish remover, shoe polish (which reminds me of church), and Lysol. He tried coffee, chocolate, tuna fish, leather, mothballs, ammonia, and cigarette butts. Also bubble gum and bourbon. And, we can all be thankful, he didn't forget maple syrup, oregano, and barbecue sauce.

Crayons are on the list. They ranked eighteenth in recognizability. Coffee was first, peanut butter second, Vick's third. Not on the list, but favorites of mine, which I would lobby for, are rubber cement (which I remember from my newspaper days), newspapers (which I remember from my paperboy days), Cutter's insect repellent, and the unique, ineffable, and memorable odor of a bar I used to frequent in New Britain, Connecticut.

I know there will be some judgment calls here. Some people will want to preserve Brut aftershave and Herbal Essence shampoo, numbers 35 and 53 on Cain's list, and I will not. Some people won't want to have fresh cow manure in the museum. I think it's a must. Some people may even want to have all the smells on aroma discs instead of having the objects themselves. Those people will not be allowed to vote. Whatever the problems are, we should start solving them now; it's time to start paying attention to our odor culture. We're responsible for what posterity will smell, and like to smell. You tend to favor the odors you grow up with. As Cain points out, why else would anyone buy Noxzema? In other words, if we're not careful, we may survive the arms race only to end up alive but befuddled in a country in which everyone thinks garden hoses are supposed to smell like cherries.

Flea-Bite Economics

There are, in the fur of America's cats and dogs, four and a half billion fleas.* They live in relative obscurity. When people think of fleas at all it's usually in terms of circuses or disease. And it's true, there was that business of the black death. Rat fleas did help kill off a quarter of the human population of Europe. But they didn't mean to. They visited the plague on our houses because they bore, unwittingly, the bacteria that cause bubonic plague. And it might be remembered, as one flea specialist has pointed out, that the black death was no party for the fleas either. As goes the host, so goes the ectoparasite. A lot of fleas died too.

Things have changed since the fourteenth century. Bu-

*Or else I miss my guess. To get this number, which would be most accurate for September, after the fleas have had all summer to multiply, I multiplied the average number of fleas on the average infested dog—50 to 75 (say 50)—by the number of pet cats and dogs in the country, 56 million dogs and 34 million cats, or a total of 90 million flea bearers, according to the Humane Society of the United States. The result is 4.5 billion fleas. Of course, not all 90 million animals have fleas. But some have more than 50. My veterinarian has seen a small cat with hundreds. And there are also the uncounted strays and feral cats and dogs, which support a vast, uncounted flea population. So, as we say in statistics, it averages out.

bonic plague isn't what it used to be, partly because one doesn't encounter the rat flea any more in polite company. One doesn't *have* fleas oneself at all (unless one goes to a flea ranch, as I did, and carries some of the livestock away with one, as I also did). One is primarily concerned with the cat flea, which shows little allegiance to its eponym and lives, willy-nilly, on cats and dogs alike, and will also have lunch on a human being when it gets the chance. This is the flea of which there are, in the U.S., four and a half billion. And this flea isn't a major health problem for human beings.

I know that this is about as faint as praise gets. "Doesn't cause bubonic plague" isn't the kind of thing you want on a letter of recommendation. But these are insects we're talking about, and the cat flea has other qualities. It has never received the recognition it deserves for its contribution to the economy. In the face of declining heavy industry in America and a trade deficit with Japan, the cat flea has stepped in to stimulate commerce, provide jobs, and support an entire new industry devoted to its destruction. Nor does it hamper productivity or destroy crops. It just bothers pets. One can even assign a dollar-and-cents value to a cat flea— well, a cents value anyway. A virgin adult goes for anywhere from a nickel to six cents on the research market. That would make the four and a half billion worth $225 million—if they were all virgins. I suppose if they were all for sale at once that would drop the price down—probably way down—but the cat flea should be proud to be worth anything.

There are about 1,600 species of flea, although most are of no economic importance. Nonetheless they do seem to attract money. Miriam Rothschild, of the British Rothschilds, has made a career of studying fleas. She has catalogued the Rothschild flea collection at the British Museum (Natural History). She has done considerable flea research, and in 1965 wrote in *Scientific American* both wittily and knowingly of fleas. She described, for example, the cat flea responding to exhalations of warm carbon dioxide to find a host, and another flea, which specializes in the large jird, "a rodent that lives in the sandy soil along the Ili River of central Asia." The jird flea can tell when a man walks by, and will "emerge and pursue him for quite a distance." A frightening thought. Rothschild also described what one might call the personality of fleas in one of the gentlest paragraphs ever written about something that has six legs and sucks blood. "Parasites," she wrote, "must be modest in their demands and unobtrusive in their ways."

True to her description, fleas don't put great demands on a host. Dogs and cats that don't develop allergies to flea saliva can support a population of fleas with relatively little discomfort. This, of course, is the opinion of human beings, who are notorious for underestimating the distress of others. Modest or not, fleas are determined. The cat flea may not walk a mile for a camel, but it will hop thirty feet for a Labrador retriever. Once it gets on the retriever it will breed at a good rate. If you start with ten female fleas, in a month you could end up with 100,000 eggs (with close to 100 percent hatchability) and 1,800 adult fleas, assuming, of course, that you've got twenty or so dogs to feed them. And these fleas wouldn't be that easy to kill. If you take a flea in your hand and try to squash it between thumb and forefinger, you won't succeed. Fleas are too well armored. You've got to get them on a hard surface and crush them with a fingernail, a knife, or, if you're in the mood, a ball-peen hammer.

Or you can use a flea spray. I don't know who invented insecticides, but some of the credit should go to the insects. And insecticides, in this case flea-icides, are important to the economy. This is the basis of flea-bite economics. I know it's hard to accept my idea. You have to change your notion of fleas, or of economics. And it's possible that there's some horrible flaw in my reasoning, but I can't find it. It seems to me that cat fleas, much like the individuals in *The Wealth of Nations,* promote the general welfare by pursuing their own bloody self-interest. Like this:

Pets get fleas. Pet owners buy flea shampoo, flea collars, flea sprays, and foggers, or "bombs," to purge afflicted houses. All of this means money pumped into the economy. To be sure, from the pet owner's point of view the money could have been better spent on hamburgers or X-rated video-tapes. But from the point of view of the economy, money is money. And in this case it's $600 million a year worth of money. That's how much consumers spend on "ectoparasit-icides" for the "companion animal market"—in other words, stuff to kill fleas and ticks on cats and dogs.

I myself have seen the innards of this companion animal flea market. I went, not wearing any kind of protective collar, to a flea ranch in Dallas. I call it a flea ranch. It calls itself the Zoecon corporation. It makes Vet-kem and Zodiac flea collars and sprays (sold through veterinarians and pet stores), and it was a Zoecon executive, who works in a shiny new granite and glass office building, who gave me the dollar figures on the flea economy. They don't keep the fleas in that building. They're on the other side of a parking lot, in a smaller building. But, then, fleas are small.

Zoecon has a small part of the flea business, but it's at the cutting edge of flea science. Carl Djerassi, a pioneer in the development of the birth control pill, was one of the founders of Zoecon, which has come up with something sim-ilar for fleas, although that product is more in the line of life control. The patented substance is a synthetic hormone called methoprene. Given in large doses at the wrong time (for the flea), it interrupts growth so that flea larvae, instead of wrapping themselves in cocoons, like butterflies, and then emerging as adults, just never grow up. They kind of fade

away. The nice thing about methoprene is that it doesn't
do the same thing to human beings.

When I visited Zoecon, about 250 people, 65 dogs, 70 cats,
and 100,000 fleas were working there. The animals are
involved in product testing and flea rearing.* The flea wran-
gler puts a herd of adult fleas on each of six cats that, at
any one time, are working as flea food. The fleas feed, mate,
and lay eggs. The eggs are collected and hatched, and the
larvae—teeny, bristly wormy things—are raised to adult-
hood on a diet of dried beef blood and Purina Cat Chow.

At the flea ranch I learned that if you want to anaesthe-
tize a flea you use carbon dioxide. A little bit excites them,
and a little bit more knocks them out. The reason for knock-
ing fleas out is that they're hard to handle when they're
awake. You can't just scoop up fifty fleas in a tablespoon
and sprinkle them on a mongrel like jimmies on ice cream.
But if you run a plastic tube from a big CO_2 tank to a jar
full of fleas, and open the valve, the fleas turn into quiescent
black dots, as docile as sand. Until they wake up. Then they
tend to jump on visitors. The man at Zoecon who conducts
the tests on dogs picked one runaway flea off my neck as
it was about to drill through my skin. When I got back to
my hotel, undressed, and shook out my clothes, another flea
leaped out. And I had no CO_2. Naked and unarmed, except
for a hotel issue plastic shoehorn, I hunted the insect down
and killed it. The process took about fifteen minutes and
would have done Chaplin proud.

I don't think I brought any fleas home with me, but since

---

*The latter, done on cats, isn't quite so bad as it sounds. Although it's
not good either. Cats that develop an allergic reaction are taken off
flea rearing for a rest, so the ones that are working aren't actually
itching all the time. You could say that at least these cats have jobs.
Not everybody can be a high-living Siamese. The cats come from the
pound and if somebody hadn't hired them, their prospects would have
been bleak. Also, they're doing their bit for cat-kind, although since
they're cats, this probably doesn't mean much to them.

I went to Zoecon, I've been troubled by something else. I made up the flea-bite economy to be funny. But Zoecon is a real company where people make real money. What if flea-bite economics isn't a joke? (I'll bet this is what happened with the supply-side theory.) I've searched for a way to disprove it. You could say that the money spent on fleas is thrown away because nothing useful is produced. But then what about the money spent on movies? Are they useful? I suppose it depends on the movie. But even the worst are good for the economy. And what about dandruff shampoos? Is dandruff good for the economy, and bad breath, and body odor, not to mention cockroaches, ants, and silverfish? Are they all good too? I think so. It seems inescapable: everything that's bad, but not that bad, for which it's possible to market a remedy is good.

As disconcerting as this idea is—both economically and grammatically—it's also reassuring. It solves a long-standing problem in theology. (They claim that science doesn't have anything to say about religion, but they're wrong.) For many years, certain people have claimed that God put everything on earth for a reason. Other people, usually adolescents, have said, "Yeah, what about fleas and dandruff?" These are things that aren't bad enough to test our souls, and nobody nowadays believes that dandruff comes from the devil (fleas maybe, but not dandruff). So why are they here? The usual answer has been that God moves in mysterious ways (like a knight in chess), and we need not understand Him, but I think even the people who take this position have always been a little embarrassed by it. Now there's a better answer. These things are on earth for a reason, and it turns out to be the same reason that everything else is here: to help us make money. So, thank God for fleas.

Welcome
to Planet Photon

OZ and I—OZ is his code name, mine is GOR—are considerably older than most of the other Photon Warriors. We're standing by our base goal, listening to a disembodied woman's voice tell us about our mission. The voice is husky, and either menacing or seductive (I always get those two confused). Most of the time I can't understand what the voice is saying, but I don't think that's supposed to be part of the game.

With our phasers at the ready, OZ and I discuss strategy. We've been getting murdered. We keep getting an awful "Buzz!" in our helmets that means we've been shot (−10 points). Usually we don't even see who's shooting us. We run, hide, spin, shoot, and what we get is more buzzes. Other people, like CD DISK, are scoring 600 or 700. We've been getting scores like 140 and −90. Not this time. This time we have a plan. At the end of the countdown we sprint to the sniper's nest. We hunker down, picking off the red team players (10 points per hit) when they come out of hiding. Sometimes we get picked off too. As the game wanes, we rush their goal (200 points if you hit it three times in a row). OZ tears down a ramp into a corridor, flattens himself against a wall, jumps out into the open, spins, shoots, gets shot. I make my dash to a tunnel, where I start getting

91

buzzes from an invisible enemy. I look for cover. Crouched in the dark, hiding, I ask myself: Is this any way for a grown man to spend Friday night? And what's my score?

Incredibly, our strategy doesn't pay off. After the game, on the big TV screen in the lobby, many lines below CD DISK, are GOR 180, and OZ 40. If you think I'm depressed, you should see OZ.

Back in the old days, before Photon, before you could get *inside* a video game, there was Asteroids, and Space Invaders, and what, for my money (and I spent enough on it), was, and still is, the greatest video game of them all— Missile Command. I can't say I was a great player. At the Times Square arcade where I spent my lunch breaks I was just a hacker. Of course, the competition was tough. Times Square is to video games what Times Square is to crime— and it's the same people who are good at both. However, once, on a trip to Brattleboro, Vermont, I played Missile Command at a little arcade, a spot of bright urban blight beeping and flashing in the midst of the health-food stores. I got the highest score the machine had ever seen, and left singing "You don't tug on a Superman's cape, you don't spit into the wind, you don't pull the mask off the old Lone Ranger, and you don't mess around with Jim." At least not in Brattleboro.

I was deeply involved in video games. I still think there's no music as sweet as the noise of the Playland arcade at 48th and Broadway with all the games going at once. It's like being in an electronic rain forest. And there's nothing like seeing that the top three scores on a game are 999,999 (as high as the counter goes), and that three players who beat the game are GEE, MAX, and GOD. When you see that you say to yourself, "This is the place."

I myself never noticed any negative effects of video games. Sometimes, after a three-hour, $15 Missile Command lunch I would feel cheap and used—not if I had a good score, though. I did stop playing, but only because I started working at home, far from the good arcades. Then, finally, I moved out of Manhattan, bought a house, and had children. I mowed the lawn. I learned how to use a screwdriver. And I took up tennis. Now that's a game that can really make you feel cheap and used.

So, when Planet Photon was born I was ripe for recruitment. Certain things were missing from my life, like sound effects. And I wasn't yet prepared to see myself as others (my neighbors) saw me: round-shouldered and beleaguered, pushing a double stroller with two kids in it, dragging along two untrained, ungroomed dogs in a circus parade of domestic confusion—in other words, as the exact opposite of Arnold Schwarzenegger. I wanted to see myself differently, as a guy in a helmet, with a phaser in his hand, zapping the Klingons. As soon as I heard about the game, I started practicing my moves.

Planet Photon was invented by George A. Carter III, the man who also invented, and I quote his news release, "the world's first motorized surfboard." Remember the motorized surfboard? No? Well, as Carter III himself has admitted, he "anticipated the market a little too soon." Ah, but then he thought of Photon, a cross between a science fiction movie and a very large video game. The promotional literature on the game mentions the movie *Tron,* a fantasy in which people enter a video game. According to Carter, with Photon, the fantasy is now reality.

Photon is played on an indoor field of 10,000 square feet. The basic field (three of the nine existing Photons have the more complex Omega field) is high-ceilinged, carpeted, and has two levels. There are ramps, tunnels, some tacky lighting, music, hidey holes, walls, base goals—pretty much anything you might want in a planet. There's also one slightly grotesque touch, a gallery, or walkway over the field, from which spectators may watch the game, or, for a dollar, use one of the gallery's phaser stations. From these stations you take target practice. You can shoot the players. But they can't shoot you.

The players must shoot each other. To this end, they're issued helmets, battery belts, chest pods, and phasers, and allowed to sign on with any code name they like, "Ace" or "Ed Norton" (who was very good) or "Fooltron" (who wasn't). There are referees to explain and enforce the rules. You're not allowed to stick your phaser through grates or around corners, run at ninety miles an hour down the ramps, or get within five feet of another player. (I'm sure full-contact Photon will evolve in the near future.) Unlike tennis, Photon has sound effects. Helmet speakers ring with zings, zaps, and buzzes when you hit or miss opponents, or get shot yourself.

Naturally, computers are involved. The scorekeeping and sound effects are managed by two IBM PCs. I suppose that, depending on your point of view and how good a shot you are, you might look on Photon as part of the humanization of technology or as just another form of electronic leprosy. I'd say that Photon is a positive contribution to human life, but not that positive. I would compare it in value to the introduction of the three-point shot in professional basketball. The difference, of course, is in the infrared light (this is what the phasers shoot, not laser beams) and the little computer chips in each player's chest pod, which register hits and communicate, by means of radio waves, with the PCs. Larry Bird, as we know, doesn't wear a chest pod, although I'm not entirely convinced that Kevin McHale isn't at least partly electronic.

I've now played Photon in Dallas, by myself, and in Kenilworth, New Jersey, with OZ. (The shooters in New Jersey are tougher, although I can't say why or Don Corleone will send somebody to break my legs.) And I'm sorry to say that

Photon is nothing at all like being in a video game. The two experiences are physically, and metaphysically, opposite. At its peak, video game play is an "out of body" experience. What happens is that after an hour or two the brain reaches a state of deep relaxation, a technologically induced trance. The mind enters the game. Like Zen archers who can hit the target blindfolded because they *are* the arrow (at least that's my idea of how they do it), you *are* the missile, or the ray, or the blip. The self disappears, along with the self's quarters. Action occurs without the usual physical limits. Maybe your fingers are limited by the speed of light, maybe not. Maybe they're your fingers, maybe not. Until you run out of change. That's when the self re-emerges and drags the fingers kicking and screaming out into the harsh and sobering light of Broadway.

Photon isn't like this. For one thing, it costs more than a quarter to play. It's $3 or more per six-and-a-half-minute game, depending on where you play, and $4.50 or more for the membership fee. More important, Photon is a decidedly in-body experience, and in my body this isn't such a great thing. If they had rented me Ivan Lendl's body (or Martina Navratilova's—what the hell, as long as it's a Czech) my scores might have been higher. But the game isn't that advanced yet. They only provide helmets and phasers. It's BYOB (bring your own body). And you never know, until you try it, what popping up and down from behind good cover and sprinting through tunnels in a modified duck walk will do to your thighs.

Thigh pain isn't the stuff of fantasy, at least not my fantasies. In Photon it's impossible to believe, for more than ninety seconds, that you're anybody other than yourself, and I can get that at home for free. It's not just the limits of your own body that serve as reminders of dull reality. There are other bodies in this game too. In particular, there are a lot of junior high school kids who sign in with names like Psychopath or Gaddafi (this kid wasn't well received in Dallas) or Lord Corwin (from a series of science fiction novels), and then wander around, chubby and befuddled, getting riddled with light beams by eighteen-year-old ne'er-do-wells who are presumably taking a break from substance abuse. Of course, the advantage to having little kids in the game is that everybody gets to shoot them. OZ, who teaches junior high school, found this particularly gratifying. And it was in the game with the kids that we both got our highest scores.

As to the effect of Photon on the kids themselves, I don't think it will rot their brains. Drugs and television will rot their brains. Infrared light is no big deal. Besides, Photon will keep them in good enough physical condition so that when they're my age they can play tennis. And I don't believe, as I'm sure somebody does, that Photon is part of the Ramboization of America. I suspect that pinging people with toy phasers is far less inducive to violence than watching one of Stallone's ketchup classics. The sad truth (for those of us who like the occasional evening on another planet) is that although there's a little shooting going on, the big difference between Photon and Capture the Flag is that Photon uses more electricity.

Nonetheless, the game seems to be a success. According to Carter III's office, 147 franchises have been sold, including the licensing of twenty playing fields in Japan. Everybody I've talked to agrees that the Japanese will love the game. Most people think it's the electronic gadgetry that will attract them. I think it's also the code names. A friend who just returned from Japan with a huge hangover told me that businessmen there, when they go drinking, use special names (not their own) so that they won't be ashamed of what they do and say. Such names are ready-made for

Photon. And once the game takes off in Japan I think we can rely on the Japanese to take it a step further and produce a street and subway version. In this game each player will carry a completely self-contained, miniaturized apparatus about the size of a portable tape player. It will be called, naturally, the Sony Hit Man.

In Vino Sanitas

I was so relieved to hear that wine is good for my health. You see I used to be a wine bore. And I never noticed that drinking did anything for my health, or my personality, although it did give me something to talk about. At the zenith of my interest in wine (which coincided with the nadir of my friends' interest in it) I could go on for minutes about the quality of the soil of Saint-Émilion and Graves, about the varieties of grape grown in the Médoc and Pomerol. I could do a complete exegesis of a German wine label. I knew what *Trockenbeerenauslese* meant, and I could say "noble rot" in three languages.* I could also talk the nonsense of the palate: I found berry in the Zinfandel, a trace of ash in the Cabernet, and, once, a suspicious hint of PCBs in an overly supple young Chardonnay from the state of Washington.

At some point, sadly, I felt I had said everything I had to say about tannin. My conversational level went straight downhill, which is to say in the direction of "drinkin' half gallons and callin' for more." This latter kind of wine talk

---

*German, *Edelfäule;* French, *pourriture noble;* and English, noble rot. *Trockenbeerenauslese* means, roughly, "selected shriveled berry picking." What that means is another story altogether.

was reported as early as the sixteenth century by that great wine writer, François Rabelais: "Page, my dear boy, fill this up till it spills over, if you please.—Wine red as a cardinal's hat! . . . Toss it off like a Breton!—Down in one gulp. That's the stuff." This account of an early wine tasting appeared in *Gargantua,* and Rabelais called it the Drunkards' Conversation. As it makes evident, without disquisitions on the aesthetics of the nose and palate, drinking wine becomes less like going to an art gallery, and more like plain old drinking. One has only the experience itself, and not the endless conversation about the experience. It hardly seems worth it.

That's why I'm so happy to see medical science enter the vineyards. I've been convinced for some time that the purpose of science is to provide something to talk about when art and poetry and music lose their appeal (and how often can you sing "Wine spo-dee-o-dee, drinkin' wine . . ."?). Now, what Masters and Johnson did for sex and Einstein did for trains, medicine has done for drinking. No longer when faced with the question of what to say about the 1980 Brane-Cantenac you're having with your carpaccio,* need you babble about why it matured earlier than the '79s, or is so much in the shadow of the massive '82s. Instead, you can raise the question of whether, as you drink it, it's increasing the level of high density lipoproteins in your blood stream to scour away the atherosclerotic plaque that the carpaccio is in the process of depositing. This is a whole new aspect of the complementarity of wine and food.

The origins of the current fascination, if not intoxication, with the idea that drinking is good for you lie in several epidemiological studies that show that people who have one

---

*Carpaccio is neither a character from *Romeo and Juliet* nor a friend of Frank Sinatra's, but raw beef sliced extremely thin and served with tasty sauces like tarragon mayonnaise.

or two drinks per day (of anything alcoholic) are likely to live longer and have fewer fatal heart attacks than people who drink a lot or people who don't drink at all. At first glance this seems like great news. There is, however, the problem of sticking to one or two drinks a day. Perhaps it takes a certain kind of person to approach alcohol in such a measured, unenthusiastic way, and it's being that person (not trying to mimic his habits) that defends against heart attacks. This person is not too tense, not too loose, not a stiff-necked teetotaler, but not someone who figures that as long as the bottle's open he might as well finish it. He's steady, unexcitable, predictable; he makes sure he gets his bran in the morning. He's able to treat a bottle of Le Montrachet (one of God's great gifts to drinkers) as if it were a dose of salts. He is, in short, a person in whom moderation has reached the level of irredeemable excess.

For those of us who aren't this person, who occasionally stray and drink three glasses in a given day, there are other good things about wine. I learned about them through the Wine Institute, an organization that works on behalf of the California wine industry. Some of these industry organizations, like the National Live Stock and Meat Board or the Tobacco Institute, are a bit biased, but I think the Wine Institute is pretty objective. Its attitude seems to be summed up by a headline in a booklet it publishes called "Wine and America." The headline reads WINE IS CIVILIZATION.

The institute recently sponsored a symposium on Wine, Health, and Society. (I didn't make it to the meeting because of a Gewürztraminer hangover, but the institute was kind enough to send me transcripts of some of the talks.) Several doctors appeared and spoke on behalf of wine, but I didn't take that too seriously. What impressed me was that Jane Brody appeared at the symposium and had good things to say about wine. Jane Brody, for those of you who haven't

been terrified by her, writes the "Ways to Die" column in
The New York Times (the newspaper calls it "Personal
Health"). Each week she writes about some new thing that
can kill you (or make you sick to your stomach) and how
to avoid it. I never remember how to avoid it: I just remember that it's going to kill me. She also writes books about
food, and I think it's fair to say that she has a more negative
view of pastrami than any other literary figure. She's very
critical of cholesterol and very much in favor of grains, the
wholer the better. I know in my bones, and in my arteries,
that she must hate carpaccio. I think of her as the Eighties'
answer to Rabelais. He says yes. She says no. Except, oddly
enough, to wine.

Now I don't want to give you the idea that she, or the
other speakers, or the Wine Institute, advocates heavy
drinking. They don't. They advocate moderation, except for
one suspicious passage on vitamins in that "Wine and
America" booklet. It begins, "Half a liter of wine (about
$4\frac{1}{2}$ four-ounce glasses) supplies the following vitamins: 5
percent RDA (recommended daily allowance) of riboflavin,
2 percent RDA of niacin . . ." and it goes on to pyridoxine,
folate, biotin, thiamine, and B_{12}. I worked this out on my
calculator. To get your daily ration of riboflavin (forget the
niacin) you've got to drink ten liters of Gallo Hearty Bur-
gundy. You could, I suppose, get some of it from food, but
when you're drinking that much it's hard to find time to
eat.

In addition to providing vitamins, wine relieves tension,
and even with the alcohol removed it helps you deal with
electric shocks. In one study referred to by Brody, rats that
were given "wine residue" (wine without the alcohol) showed
reduced sensitivity to shocks, as did rats that guzzled real
wine. Furthermore, moderate drinking (of any kind of alcohol) increases the levels of high density lipoproteins. We

don't know yet if these are the *good* high density lipoproteins, the ones that fight cholesterol, but I figure it's better
to be safe than sorry. Wine promotes absorption of nutrients
from food, and wine seems to show anti-viral activity. I also
believe it has a positive effect on wit. While driving through
New York's Bowery the other day (where the so-called winos
hang out) I was approached by a man who had clearly over-
indulged in some lesser vintage of Night Train or Thun-
derbird. He had a cardboard sign with the plea, "I owe
$250,000 in back rent, and I'm a quarter short."

Not only is wine good, it's better than hard liquor or beer.
John De Luca, president of the Wine Institute, has proposed
a health and safety index for alcoholic beverages to replace the old "alcohol equivalence" in which a beer equals
a shot equals a glass of wine. Wine, as he would have it, is
just not a boozer's drink. It's the "beverage of moderation."
Its alcohol is absorbed into the blood stream more slowly
than that of hard liquor. And it plays a different role in
society than other beverages that produce what one physician at the symposium referred to (condescendingly, I
thought) as "the effect of alcohol on the central nervous
system." De Luca mentions, for example, "wine's sacred
place in Catholic and Jewish religious ceremonies." A good
point. I can't see Miller Lite at a seder. And I know that
none of us would want to see John Paul II holding up a
frosted glass of pilsner in St. Peter's Basilica during the
transubstantiation.

Since wine is so good, I don't see how I can afford not to
drink. If I suffer from a little hangover, the viruses are
suffering too. And if I lose on heart attack prevention because I drink a bit too much, I nonetheless gain tremendously in reduced sensitivity to electric shock.

I didn't know about all these benefits a few years ago
when I was a member of a wine appreciation group. It wasn't
a big group, like the Society of Medical Friends of Wine or

Les Amis du Vin, or *Les Grands Chevaliers du Tastevin.* It consisted of myself and two friends and it was dissolved after two meetings for gross lack of moderation and failure to stick to the point during the discussions. But now that we have some new stuff to talk about I'd like to revive it, and rename it. In the past we called ourselves *Les Grands Amis des Chevaliers du Tastevin mit Prädikat.** I think it should now be called *Les Grands Amis des Chevalier du Tastevin mit High Density Lipoproteins.*

And the next time we meet, after we inhale the bouquet, check the wine's legs, swirl the stuff around in our mouths and swallow it, our conversation will be nothing like that of Rabelais's drunkards, but more along lines that the Wine Institute would approve of: "Could you pour a little more? I'm short on my niacin.—I like it. Very robust chromium content.—Hey, good silicon.—All right! Let's drink to magnesium absorption!—Here's to bioavailability!—The Framingham study!—Zinc!—You know what I like about this wine?—What?—The effect of its alcohol on my central nervous system, that's what. Pass the carpaccio."

---

*The Big Friends of the Knights of the Little Silver Cup with a Predicate.

Personology Today

I used to think that *Tropical Fish Hobbyist* was a great magazine. Before that I liked *Fly Fisherman, The New Yorker,* and the *Paris Review.* When I was even younger, there was *Field & Stream* and *Boys' Life,* which always had great articles on how to build things (tables, chairs, small buildings) with a jackknife. All that's behind me now. I've found a magazine that has it all, and more. It's got poetry, it's got drama, it gives you a glimpse of a strange world. It's even got good advertisements. It's called the *Journal of Personality* and I don't think anyone can afford not to subscribe, even if it does cost $27 for four issues.

I was led to the *Journal* because of a news report of some new findings (by psychologists) on love. I always like to see what happens when scientists step onto the poets' turf. In this case I found two love papers, both of them in prose, but with some nice turns of phrase, such as the description of genuine love as a "rare expression of optimal functioning . . ." and even better the reference to "Love items with rotated factor loadings." (I love it when they talk that way.)

In one of the articles there was also a sensible use of a quotation from Shakespeare. I can't tell you how rare this is. Scientists love to quote Shakespeare, but they almost always do it badly. The usual trick is for an ear, nose, and throat man to dig up a line like, "I'll speak in a monstrous little voice" (from *A Midsummer Night's Dream*, of course), and slap it on top of his latest paper on laryngitis. Well, David McClelland of Harvard firmly anchored his quote in the text of his paper for the *Journal*, and it was right on target: ". . . Love is not love/ Which alters when it alteration finds,/ Or bends with the remover to remove:/ Oh no! it is an ever-fixed mark,/ That looks on tempests and is never shaken" (Sonnet 116). McClelland was arguing, as was Shakespeare, for a view of love as characterized by joy, constancy, and altruism.

I admit that in and of themselves a couple of good phrases and some poetry aren't going to pull readers away from *Fly Fisherman*. And the *Journal* does have some real drawbacks. There are no photographs, which puts it at a disadvantage to more colorful publications. But, having looked through a number of issues, I can tell you that it does what all great magazines do: it expands your awareness. Four times a year it brings into your home (as magazine publishers love to say) the world of psychology, a world that is, in its own way, every bit as exotic as that of the angelfish or the largemouth bass.

The words psychologists use are themselves worth the price of a subscription. These are words you don't see anywhere else, like "personologist." I don't have enough room to quote the title of the article in which this word appears, but the paper is about how the non-psychologist, you or I, makes judgments about people he meets. Everybody does this of course, but in the transforming language of psychology, everybody becomes an "intuitive personologist."

This is a matter of style. The content is even more intriguing. I don't mean the conclusions the scientists come to, which aren't so interesting, but how they get to those conclusions, how psychologists work. I never knew that in a lot of these studies, students are required to be experimented on in order to get course credit. For instance, in a breakthrough study on fidgeting, which I'll discuss in detail later, "students participated in the study as part of a course requirement." In other cases students "volunteer," but get partial course credit for that invaluable part of any liberal arts education: being an experimental subject.

The way I read it, this means that a practicing academic psychologist can get tenure, write a textbook, and then teach a course in which students are required not only to buy his book but also to be subjects for whatever experiments he wants to do on them. Usually the kids just have to answer questionnaires. But not always. In a study at the University of Toronto on candy eating (published, I'm sorry to say, in a competing journal) subjects were "pre-loaded," which means that they had to drink not one, but two eight-ounce Borden milkshakes, one chocolate and one vanilla, *before* they started eating the candy. Is this any way to treat the daughters (all the subjects were female) of the middle class? Isn't this what convicts are for?

If the milkshake business seems gruesome, it's nothing to the work on fidgeting. Until recently, I was unaware of the large body of work on fidgeting (why people fidget, how people fidget, who fidgets). Fortunately, "An Analysis of Fidgeting and Associated Individual Differences" by Albert Mehrabian and Shari L. Friedman of UCLA, published in the June 1986 issue of the *Journal,* had a little review of some of the classic work. Jones, for instance, in 1943 "required subjects, male and female, to drink 10 glasses of water over a two-hour period while strongly discouraging their use of bathroom facilities during this period." You may wonder what happened. Surprisingly enough, "for subjects who did not use the bathroom facilities, there was a significant increase in nervous movements, particularly in the genital and leg areas, compared with subjects in the control group who simply rested for two hours." Yet other researchers, forgoing the water treatment, had a system in which schizophrenic patients earned pennies (of course this was in 1973, when a penny was a penny) on a "fixed interval schedule," which I take to mean that every so many minutes the sane person gave the crazy person a penny. Well, when the researchers started taking longer to give out the pennies, the poor schizophrenics showed "increased pacing and water consumption," as you can well imagine. Unfortunately, the researchers didn't think to capitalize on this serendipitous turn of events and take the study one step further by discouraging the schizophrenics' use of bathroom facilities. Too bad. When opportunities like this are missed in science, they seldom arise again.

For their work, Mehrabian and Friedman took a new tack, using neither water nor schizophrenics. In three separate studies, they got bunches of undergraduates together and gave them questionnaires about fidgeting. In one of the studies they also had someone play checkers with each subject and take a long time to make the moves while someone else watched to see if the subject fidgeted. (Of course, one never tells the subjects the truth about what's going on, for obvious reasons. If the schizophrenics knew what the penny thing was all about that would have influenced their actions, one way or another.) On the questionnaires were statements like "I scratch myself a lot; I usually jiggle my pen when I am holding it, but not when writing with it; I often bite my lip (on purpose); I hardly ever suck on my tongue." I could tell from the questions that I'm a fidgety person. I jiggle my pens, and chew them and my fingernails, and grind my teeth. However, I want to make one thing clear. I don't suck my tongue. That's disgusting. Sometimes these kinds of studies don't come up with firm or comprehensible findings. But the last sentence of this paper is pretty clear. It says the studies led to "the conclusion that fidgety persons were either of an anxious or a hostile temperament type." So now we know.

There's a lot of competition in the magazine business. And nowhere is this more true than among journals of personality. I mentioned that the candy study wasn't reported in the *Journal of Personality*. It appeared in the *Journal of Personality and Social Psychology*. I'll call these *JP* and *JPSP*. There are others, too, like *JSP*, the *Journal of Social Psychology*, and *JPA*, the *Journal of Personality Assessment*, but you have to draw the line somewhere and I think two of these journals are enough for anyone. *JP* is my favorite. I would put its fidgeting article up against anything in *JPSP*, including the milkshake/candy article, and even including the astonishing "Presidential Personality" paper by Dean Keith Simonton of the University of California, Davis, in the July 1986 issue.

To gauge the personalities of the thirty-nine U.S. presidents, Simonton, who calls his field "historiometry," gathered together biographical material—in other words, things that other people had written about the presidents—and put it all on index cards. Then, for each president, "raters" read the cards (without knowing which president was being described in a given set of cards) and decided which of 300 adjectives applied. Through methods too mysterious to recount here, the 300 adjectives were divided into fourteen categories, each rated numerically to tell us things like who was the tidiest president (Buchanan) and how many of the thirty-nine showed less intellectual brilliance than Ronald Reagan. (The answer, which says something about American history, or "historiometry," is twenty-five.)

Now, I know Simonton couldn't interview the thirty-nine

presidents, or preload them with milkshakes. Most of them
are dead. And it would have been silly to have studied what
they wrote themselves since these days a president would
no more write his own speeches than he would iron his own
shirts. I was, however, surprised to read that dozens of the
"descriptors" from the list were *"prima facie"* useless because they didn't apply that well to any president. Among
these adjectives were: cruel, fickle, foolish, obnoxious, and
whiny. This made me wonder whether we were talking
about the same presidents.

Whoever these guys are, Simonton's method produced
some remarkable conclusions about them. Lyndon Johnson,
who showed his abdominal scars to the world and had his
advisers attend him as he sat on the toilet, was much tidier
than John Kennedy. Eisenhower was enormously dumber
than Ronald Reagan, who is just as smart as Richard Nixon.
And Kennedy ties with Millard Fillmore for second on
the most attractive. Franklin Pierce beat them both by a
nose.

This is good stuff. And it may seem that between *JP* and
JPSP it's hard to pick a winner, but that's only until you
look at the advertisements. The best one I found in *JPSP*
had to do with how to get grants. But on the back cover of
JP's love issue there was a pitch for psychological testing
kits that brought back to me those great ads in *Boys' Life*
and *Field & Stream,* the ones for taxidermy courses, body
building, and worm farms. The *JP* advertisement was from
Psychological Test Specialists of Missoula, Montana, which
sounds to me like the place the taxidermy courses used to
come from. The tests that looked good to me were "Proverbs
Test (PT)," billed as a "Highly sensitive indicator of psy-
chotic processes. $13.00 for kit" and the "Famous Sayings
(FS)" test, also $13.00, in which "Agreement with proverbs,
aphorisms, and folk sayings is analyzed to determine per-

sonality structure. Particularly useful in personnel selection." (All work and no play makes Jack a dull boy. Do you agree?) I'm very tempted to send away for them. The writing business is always shaky and I'd like to have a little something on the side. A little psychological testing, a worm farm, maybe some taxidermy—I think I could make a go of it.

Ecology Quinella

Remember ecology? Back when Earth Day and tie-dyed shirts and noncompetitive sports (was it hug ball they all played?) were in vogue, ecology was big. Of course, it's still big to ecologists, who never seem to tire of doing complicated mathematical analyses of the rises and falls of various aphids and beetles. (Remember Japanese beetles?) But as a buzzword, it has lost its buzz. It has been squeezed out of the public consciousness by investment banking and tax-free municipal bonds.

I suspect that the reason is the granola factor. I was talking to my seventeen-year-old nephew the other day and I heard him call some poor girl he'd met on a bus trip a "granola." I asked him what he meant. As you might expect, granolas are people who are overly devoted (in the opinion of non-granolas) to things like natural foods and organic gardening. By the process of metonymy, granolas have come not to be, but to be called, what they eat. I think that ecology, like my nephew's bus companion, smacks of granola, and granola isn't the thing to smack of in the eighties. Among today's celebrities there are very few granolas. Jello Biafra, who sings with a group called the Dead Kennedys, is almost certainly not a granola. Ronald Reagan and Donald Trump aren't granolas. Don Johnson doesn't even eat

111

breakfast. I'm not a granola (of course I'm not a celebrity either), although I do have certain granola-like attitudes. I eat oatmeal, for instance, and I've been thinking about gardening organically.

Ecology may also be a "retro" science, but this I'm not sure about. I'm also not sure whether being retro is good or bad. I do know that it's a word worth looking into. The same week I heard my nephew use it, I saw it in the *New York Review of Books,* although there it wasn't in English. Someone was describing nostalgia as *le goût rétro.*

Certainly ecology, in its obsessive preoccupation with untouched nature, seems to have a taste for the past, and I don't mean the twenties and thirties, I mean the Mesozoic, when mammals were in no position to build power plants, and if there was any toxic waste it was presumably natural and in its proper place. The example of an ecosystem given to students is hardly ever the Bronx or Atlantic City. It's always that primeval pond. Remember the pond? Every student of ecology has had to hear about the algae and phytoplankton and fish and turtles. This pond is very old by now, also mucky, what my nephew would call rude. When human beings do enter the picture they always seem to be wearing a loincloth or toting wooden hoes. They live in villages, or travel in nomadic groups that treat the deer and the bear with the kind of totemic respect we reserve for the deutschmark and the yen. Perhaps the most famous of these villages is a hypothetical one that appeared in a parable by Garrett Hardin. He made it up to illustrate the problems of population growth and limited resources. In his pastorale, villagers share a common on which they graze their cattle. If they don't limit the growth of the herds all the cattle die. This is a good story, but out of date. Some cities, like Boston, still have commons, but grazing isn't what gets done on them.

If ecology is to regain its former position in society, it

needs a new image, something with a little snap to it, like mens' underwear for women. The image I have in mind is that of a racetrack. I think the racetrack could be the new controlling model in ecology. To explain why, I have a story to tell about racetracks, a kind of parable. Hardin called his the Tragedy of the Commons. I call mine the Comedy of the Horse Manure. Like most comedies, it isn't that funny to the people who are in it, but at least in this one the animals don't die.

Once, not too long ago, mushrooms thrived in the land of Pennsylvania, near Kennett Square. They were grown in the traditional medium of choice for mushrooms—composted horse manure. Fortunately there were a lot of horses in neighboring lands, at racetracks like Aqueduct and Belmont where the ponies raced and sharpies in white shoes placed bets at the $50 windows. As a natural consequence of all these horses the racetracks had enormous amounts of horse manure. People came up from Pennsylvania, manure haulers by trade, and paid good money for this manure, which made the racetrack people chuckle with delight. Of course the haulers chuckled too, because they turned around and sold the manure to the mushroom growers, again for good money. The growers, as you have probably guessed, also chuckled, because they sold their mushrooms for even better money.

One day, mushrooms from afar (Taiwan, China, Korea) arrived in cans and took over big chunks of the market for mushrooms in cans—the precise market in which many growers in Pennsylvania sold their mushrooms. Suddenly the money was not as good. The growers suffered, the haulers of manure suffered, and the tracks had to pay to have the horse manure taken away. Everybody at all ends of the manure business was unhappy, except one clever man who found a way out of this slough of manure and despond—a new way to sell the product. He turned it into compost right at the racetrack and sold it to garden centers, nurserymen, and landscapers so that it would grow not mushrooms but tomatoes, zucchini, privet hedges, and dwarf conifers. Once again the sharpies could place their bets at the $50 windows without undue worry about where the manure from all the longshots was going.

My parable happens to be true. The mushrooms are real. The manure is real. The track is real. It's the Saratoga Raceway in Saratoga, New York. This isn't the flat track where thoroughbred horses race every August and pedigreed humans show up in fancy straw hats and boaters. This is a harness track, open year-round, where the hat of choice is a baseball cap, preferably emblazoned with the name of some maker of heavy machinery. The clever man is Robert W. Morris. He didn't actually invent composting, but he did study it and experiment with different methods. He even went to visit what may be the world center of composting knowledge, the U.S. Department of Agriculture sludge composting operation in Beltsville, Maryland. Then, finally, he spent $225,000 to put together his own system. It turns the manure output of 1,100 trotters and pacers, which, mixed with the straw and sawdust from the stalls, amounts to 150 cubic yards a day, into rich, crumbly compost, what James Crockett, the garden guru, calls brown gold.

Before he set the system up, the track was paying $100,000 a year to get the stuff hauled away. Now it takes in $300,000 a year. Morris even mixes the clay and sand he scrapes off the track during maintenance with the compost to make topsoil, which he also sells. And he keeps down the flies by buying wasps that eat fly eggs—organic all around. Other tracks are following his lead. According to Morris, Keeneland in Kentucky has built a plant, Charles Town in West Virginia is building one, and a number of other tracks, including the Meadowlands in New Jersey, are studying the operation. Morris sells his plans and expertise for $10,000.

It seems to me that my parable, like Hardin's, has an ecological moral, which is that if we ran the planet the way Morris runs his raceway we'd be in a lot better shape. And we could do it. This isn't some imaginary village we're talking about; there are no aborigines living in an unspoiled wilderness in this story. This is spoiled wilderness—a harness track, not far from a major highway. This is no fantasy, it's a business. Here's an efficient, elegant, ecologically sound operation that was developed not out of a sense of oneness with all life, but for the sake of *money*. This is the heart of the harness track story in terms of public appeal. Nothing, but nothing, is less like granola than money.

I suppose there might be some question about whether the racetrack can replace the old pond as a model ecosystem. I don't see why not. A racetrack operation is built on the $2 bettor, whom we might compare to photosynthetic phytoplankton, or algae. In the pond the plankton and algae capture the energy of the sun and form the base of the food chain. At the track the $2 bettors do something similar. They provide the money. The parimutuel betting system, through which this money flows, guarantees that all life forms at the track are interdependent, as in natural ecosystems. If Coup de Fusil is 2 to 1 on the morning line but the bettors are putting most of their money on other horses, the odds increase to 4 to 1. Every bettor and horse is connected to every other bettor and horse.

In the pond, sunlight is transformed into vegetation, vegetation into animals, and those animals into bigger animals as one thing eats another. At the track, money is transformed into fancy cars, stocks and bonds, and more horses. Of course these stocks and bonds don't go to the phytoplankton. It's the large mammals at the top of the chain, the owners and (sometimes) the big bettors, who get rich. However, as with the familiar carbon and nitrogen cycles, something trickles back to the small fry to keep the system going. The $2 bettor may be largely excluded from the big money, but, at least at Saratoga Raceway, he can still get in on the manure. One hundred twenty pounds, already composted, costs just $5 at a local garden center.

Good scientific models have wide applications, and I think the racetrack could subsume the ecology and evolution of all life on earth. Science fiction writers are fond of speculating that the planet is a zoo maintained by higher intelligences. It works better as a racetrack. I figure the creatures who run it are strange energy conglomerations with cigars and white shoes who lounge around saying stuff like "I'll take the mammals in the Pleistocene," or "I like the hadrosaurs in the late Cretaceous." If this is true the question of interest to us has to be what the morning line is on human beings. I suspect we're a long shot, good in the first few furlongs but easy prey to a dark horse (or insect) like the cockroach because of our tendency to blow ourselves up in the stretch.

Still, long shots do come in now and then. Love Champ did. I couldn't visit the composting operation without going to the track, so on the day I went to Saratoga I spent the afternoon with the runners and the evening with the trotters, doing research. (I won two daily doubles and two quinellas and came out $40 ahead for the day. If you care to send me your money I'll be happy to invest it for you.) At the harness track, after looking over the past performances, I put $2 to win on Love Champ in the first. She surged ahead at the wire and paid 10–1. I also bought some Saratoga Organic that day, and later I worked it into my garden. The way I see it, Love Champ not only won me $20 but next spring she's going to make my tomatoes grow. Now that's ecology.

Planet of the Evangelists

Sometimes I think the scientific establishment is too hard on creationists. They're not so bad. For one thing, they've got a sense of humor. The only way that I can see that the Bible can be literally true, and the planet thousands and not billions of years old, is that the entire geological column and the fossil record are part of a practical joke perpetrated by You Know Who. As jokes go, I like it. Imagine: a God who antiques planets just to confuse the inhabitants.

In literary terms we might think of this God as an unreliable narrator. And it's clear to me, if not to the creationists, that if He'd fool around with thousands of feet of rock just to trick us, He might also have stuck a few fibs in the Bible. Could it be that He's just teasing us about the seven days, the way He did with that bit about Jonah and the whale?

Looked at in this light the creation/evolution conflict is good fun—as conflicts go—certainly better than, say, a *thermonuclear* conflict, or the Super Bowl. This is the way I try to look at it anyway. I enjoy watching the creationists attack the fundamental basis of biological science and the evolutionists argue that whoever wrote the Bible wasn't versed in molecular biology. It tickles me to hear the claims on both sides about threats to morality, religion, the Constitution, and the minds and/or souls of our young people. Nonetheless, every once in a while, I get angry too. What gets me is when they start picking on the apes.

When *The Origin of Species* first hit the bookstores ape jokes were very big. Ape cartoons of Darwin were all the vogue, and the pugnacious T. H. Huxley, who often served as Darwin's front man, was asked, at a meeting of the British Association in 1860, on which side he was descended from an ape, his mother's or his father's. You'd think that things would have changed, now that apes have learned language, and star in one television program after another. But they still get no respect. Just recently a witness in one of these endless creationist court cases (this one is on its way to the Supreme Court) came up with this tired old saw: "I think if you teach children that they are evolved from apes, they will start acting like apes."

Well, really. Never mind that apes and human beings are actually descended from another creature. That's just evolutionist nitpicking. The point is that we're obviously related to apes, as anyone knows who has ever taken a good look at a chimpanzee's fingers. It's equally obvious that we act like them and always have, no matter who or what we think our ancestors are.* It's easier now than ever before to prove this contention, because we have definitive information on precisely how at least some apes act. We have the recently published and thoroughly impressive *The Chimpanzees of Gombe* by Jane Goodall, a 673-page masterwork in which Goodall does for Gombe what Joyce did for Dublin.

The chimps have their bad moments, it's true—murder, rape, infanticide, cannibalism—but nobody's perfect. On

---

*And sometimes we act *with* them, as in *Bedtime for Bonzo*.

the positive side, they usually care for their children, are very social, engage in coordinated group hunts, and have brief sexual affairs in which the male and female go off together for a weekend or more to the Gombe equivalent of a country inn—a tree perhaps, or a glade. The chimps form friendships. Brothers and sisters, and brothers and brothers, forge lifelong bonds. They're always grooming each other, to the point they sometimes seem to be an entire species of hairdressers. And most impressive of all, they have a rudimentary political system. The group is dominated by an alpha male, who's periodically challenged by aspiring leaders. Traditionally, leadership is gained and maintained by strongmen (strongchimps?) who form coalitions with other apes. There are also times of instability, when no ape reigns. It's just like South America.

If this isn't enough to prove how much alike we are, consider the astonishing evidence among the Gombe chimps of rudimentary shopping behavior. For instance, they test fruits they're about to eat by squeezing and sniffing them. And once they've brought a piece of fruit home, or at least picked it, they have what you might call recipes, established ways to prepare and eat different kinds of food. They don't write these recipes down, but we can.

Fig Leaves

Pick the leaves one by one. Pile together. Fold them over and chew well.

Aspilia Leaves

Press and rub against the palate. Do not chew.

These may not be up to Escoffier's standards, but if you've ever seen a dog eat you know that by comparison chimps are well on the road to the perfect omelette. They even have cultural differences in cuisine. The Gombe chimps feed on various parts of the oil-nut palm. But a nearby group, the Mahale chimpanzees, won't touch it. Goodall doesn't suggest that this is the result of a religious prohibition, however, merely a matter of taste and custom.

I know what the creationists are going to say to all this. They're going to say that I've forgotten something of supreme importance. Human beings have souls and chimpanzees don't. Well, a soul is a hard thing to measure. On a more concrete but still soul-related level, human beings also have churches and preachers. I can't honestly say that chimpanzees go to church (in the wild), but preachers are another matter. I can show that preachers and chimpanzees are quite a lot alike. In fact, since Goodall has given us abundant evidence in her opus of the individuality of each ape, I can go beyond this generalization. I can say which preacher is like which ape.

Remember now, I'm not saying these guys are chimps, just that they're like chimps in certain ways, almost all of them complimentary. It so happens the preachers I have in mind are both well-known television evangelists. This is only fair. If you're going to compare religious leaders to chimpanzees you've got to go for the big ones. I had thought of doing the pope, but Roman Catholic theology is so hospitable to evolution that it takes the fun out of it. As far as we know, John Paul II would have no objection to being linked (biologically) to other primates.*

---

*Darwin himself was almost a preacher. During his youth he sowed his wild oats by studying for the ministry. Of course he later settled down and became an evolutionist, or perhaps I should say *the* evolutionist. Darwin's father (the ministry was his idea) must have seen it coming. He said to his son once, "You care for nothing but shooting, dogs, and rat-catching, and you will be a disgrace to yourself and all your family."

I'm not at all sure that the two preachers I've picked will take the comparison with the same good grace one expects from the pontiff. They're Jimmy Swaggart and Pat Robertson. The latter has the added attraction of wanting to be President, which is very similar to being alpha chimp in Gombe. Jimmy Swaggart recently gave his support to Robertson's presidential quest, but that's not why I picked him. I picked Swaggart because he's my all-time favorite television evangelist. I watch him whenever I get the chance. Jimmy Swaggart is running for prophet, not President. He sweats, shouts, calls out the evolutionists, and has a stage presence that would've done Elvis proud. Now, we all know that chimpanzees jump around, thump their chests, and run at each other. Of course the chimps do this to show how tough they are, while Jimmy Swaggart swaggers and shouts to show how tough God is. Nonetheless, if you read Goodall you'll be compelled to view Jimmy Swaggart as the human equivalent of Goliath.

To quote Goodall. "He [Goliath] was aggressive and had a very fast, spectacular charging display, coupled with an unusually bold disposition. If the adult males were confronted by some strange object (such as a dead python), Goliath was generally the first or only male to approach closely." You shake a dead python at Pat Robertson, he might hesitate. Jimmy Swaggart is going to jump up, praise the Lord, and rip that snake right out of your hand. Then he's going to let you have a few choice verses about serpents—in the teeth. Goliath was in his time an alpha male, so I hope Jimmy Swaggart will see the comparison as a kind of honor, and not take offense at being compared to an ape who was named for an unbeliever.

Robertson is a bit more difficult because of his lack of emotion. I'm not saying he's completely without life. He's just—well, he's the Merv Griffin of religion. He smiles no matter what he's saying. He's perfectly suited to television, and television has brought him to prominence. He developed the Christian Broadcasting Network, and is the host of its flagship show, "The 700 Club," which is a lot like Merv except that David Brenner is never on. It's Robertson's mastery of the cool medium of television that suggests which chimp he's like: Mike.

I didn't pick this chimp just to work an old Pat-and-Mike (or Pat-is-Mike) joke. Among the chimpanzees of Gombe, Mike did much the same thing Robertson is attempting to do. He was cool. He never actually attacked anybody. He got to be the alpha male by mastering a new medium. Of course in his case political prominence came from the mastery not of the airwaves but of empty kerosene cans. Mike could charge down a hill, tumbling these awful-sounding cans before him, and scare the pants, if they had any, off every ape in the neighborhood.

I'm not suggesting that just because Mike got to be president of the Gombe chimps, Robertson is going to get to be our President. In some ways, people are considerably more clever than chimpanzees. All I'm saying is that Pat Robertson is a chimpanzee's relative, and acts like one, as do we all. (I want to point out that I didn't use the word uncle, and that not even the creationists confuse monkeys and apes.)

There's a political as well as a scientific lesson in all of this. It's always important, whether you're a human being or a chimpanzee, to look beyond the kerosene cans and the camera angles. For instance, I myself am a single-issue voter. My issue is apes. The apes are my relatives, I'm proud to have them, and I don't intend to vote for anybody who isn't related to them, or is ashamed to admit it. I have one question for each presidential candidate, and I think it's a question everybody should want to know the answer to: Are you kin to the apes or not? Once we know, we'll know how to vote.

This Little Piggy

They wouldn't let me see the micro pig. It may seem that this is of importance only to me, and perhaps to the pig, but I think we all have a stake (or perhaps a chop) in this conflict. The public has a right to know about the micro pig. As a member of the press, if not the working press, I represent the public. If I don't get to see the pig, who does?

It's not as if "micro pig" were the name of some new missile. We've long since passed the stage when we gave cute names like Fat Man to nuclear weapons. (If there were a Nobel Prize for bad taste, surely the guy who came up with that one would win it.) These days technology is dominant, and it provides, rather than suffers, nicknames. Consider the Refrigerator, the first home appliance to play in the Super Bowl.

No, the micro pig isn't a bomb. It's a pig. A tiny pig. Of course you can't call it a tiny pig. Then it would sound like something from a children's story instead of a Swine Research Laboratory. In science, there are no little piggies. When pigs get little, they become mini. When they get really little, they become micro. Soon, no doubt, this gradual swine reduction program will culminate in the long-awaited laptop pig.

123

In actual avoirdupois, the measuring system traditionally favored for pork, an adult micro pig weighs 50 to 100
pounds. A mini pig weighs 150 to 200 pounds, and a serious,
old-fashioned, mainframe pig goes 600 to 800 pounds. My
own personal pig equivalence chart produces the following
equations: One regular pig equals two Refrigerator Perrys
and change. One Yucatán mini pig (that's where they come
from) equals one place kicker. One Refrigerator equals at
least three micro pigs. Of course these comparisons aren't
really fair. In the NFL, pigs don't get to carry the ball; they
are the ball.

Still, tinyness—or micro-ness, if we must—is no reason
to keep the pig hidden. What could there possibly be about
a small pig that would make someone refuse to show it to
me? This isn't Mikhail Gorbachev's tiny pig. It's not Deng
Xiaoping's pig, destined for tiny, Communist moo shu pork.
It's not even the Pentagon's pig, unfortunately.

Can you imagine what someone could charge the Defense
Department for a micro pig? It could change the economy
of rural America. But that's wishful thinking. This isn't a
war pig. This is a peace pig, bred for medical research. One
of the rules of science is that the smaller the experimental
animal, the better. Hence the popularity of fruit flies and
mice. At 800 pounds, the classic pig is unwieldy, to say the
least. The Yucatán mini pig, which nature itself produced,
was a step in the right direction. Then came the micro pig,
developed through selective breeding by Linda Panepinto
at the Miniature Swine Research Laboratory of Colorado
State University in Fort Collins.

As soon as I read about this pig, I wanted to see it. I
called Panepinto to set up an appointment. I was frank with
her. I told her that I wasn't the least bit interested in the
pig's usefulness to research, in how it was bred, or in whom
it would cure, but only in how small it was. Panepinto was

not overly enthusiastic about this approach to her work, but she was game. I made my airplane reservations and checked the map to see where I could go trout fishing when I was out there. (How long can you spend looking at a pig?) I sharpened my pencils and packed my fly rod. And then she canceled. I was aghast. The powers-that-be in the university, not Panepinto herself, had ruled that I was not to see the pig. They didn't want publicity—at least not from me. The reason? According to Panepinto, they were worried about animal rights activists. I suppose they were afraid I'd write some headline like: "Incredibly Cute Tiny Pig Destined for Vivisection."

Of course I never planned to write a headline like that. The thought had never crossed my mind. At least not until that telephone conversation, not until I felt the meat locker chill and heard, in Panepinto's voice, the dull thud of the Pork Curtain as it fell, encircling Colorado State like some vast and impenetrable side of ribs.

This has to give anyone in the press, or the pig business, pause. It raises certain questions, first among them being: How big is the pig really? I've seen a picture of one posed with a young woman, a researcher at Colorado State, but there's such a thing as trick photography. And even if the photography is accurate, who's to say that we're looking at a small pig and not at a giant person? That would explain the university's nervousness. There are restrictions about experimenting on people. You can't grow a scientist who's twenty feet tall and expect the National Science Foundation to look the other way. But I doubt Colorado State would try that. Even behind the Pork Curtain you couldn't keep a twenty-foot-tall woman a secret.

So let's stipulate the tiny pig, and assume widespread fear at Colorado State that the animal will be perceived by certain groups as just too cute for research. That's still not a reason to keep me away; I'm not part of the animal rights movement. It would be disingenuous of me, having made my peace with roast pork and barbecued ribs, to complain about a few experiments (as long as they use mesquite wood). And besides, as I understand it, these pigs (there are now a number of them) are useful because, among other things, they're susceptible to ulcers and atherosclerosis. Human beings stand in line at restaurants waiting to pay to get atherosclerosis. This is hardly what I'd call vivisection.

No, what I think Colorado State was afraid of was that I would make people understand how small a micro pig really is, and how contrary petiteness is to the nature of pigs. Somebody at Colorado State must have realized that if I were allowed to see the micro pig, and tell the world about it, I would have been able to set off a groundswell of protest and outrage that would have swamped the Miniature Swine Research Laboratory. You see, my beef with science (I've got a regular meat loaf going here) isn't that they use animals in experiments, but that they make them look silly. My position is this: Experiment on them if you have to, but leave them their self-respect. If I ever get anyone else to join me in this position, I plan to call us the Animal Dignity Movement.

It's not just pigs. Think of all the poor fruit flies with crinkly wings. And mice. I don't mean the millions we kill each year in research. I kill almost as many in mousetraps in one cabin in upstate New York. (I figure dying in traps is a noble end for mice. And noble or not, if they want to leave turds in my silverware drawer, they'll have to take their chances.) The fates worse than mousetraps that I'm thinking of involve not pain but ugliness and incompetence. Scientists have bred super-obese mice that can hardly move, naked mice that have no fur, mice that can't smell, mice that can't walk a straight line. You can even cross some of these strains and get, for example, a fat naked mouse. I hate those.

You can't build a mass movement around the humiliation of flies and rodents, but pigs are different. People care about pigs. There's a whole pig *thing* in this country. There are piggy banks, and porcelain pigs that aren't banks, not to mention Miss Piggy and the swine flu. People have been called pigs for their table manners and their politics, sexual and otherwise. In 1968, in Chicago, a swine named Pigasus was nominated for President. Some people keep pigs as pets, and other people race them. Racing pigs are set loose on a track to gallop, not for the gold, but for an Oreo cookie. Pigs today are probably the most highly cathected of farm animals.

And what, of all piggy characteristics, has given the animal such a secure seat on the *zeitgeist?* The answer is size. I've seen pigs in the pork—real, mud-covered, adult pigs— and they're nothing if not huge. They're immense. They're fat. They're round. They snort. They are, in a word that incarnates the culmination of swinehood to which every piglet aspires, hogs. That's the true destiny of pigs, but it's a destiny denied to the little piggies at Colorado State. At fifty or so pounds they might make the cutest little Canadian bacon anyone has ever seen, and help cure heart disease to boot, but they can never, ever be hogs. I find that sad.

If I'd been to see the micro pig, I might have been able to make something out of all this. I could have really stirred things up. Alas, it wasn't to be. The people at Colorado State saw me coming. They put a lid on me, all right. It's not fair. Colorado State is a public institution that uses a lot of public money, and it shouldn't shut science writers out of the pig process. But I don't know what to do about it. Maybe a letter campaign would help. Maybe it would be good if there were a spontaneous outpouring of support (for both me and the micro pig) in the form of telegrams and letters.* After all, it's not only the First Amendment to the Constitution that's at issue here. They ruined my fishing trip.

*The address is: Department of Public Information, Colorado State University, Fort Collins, CO 80523.

Paradise Lost

I had a few antiques shipped to me the other day. One of them, a Calville Blanc, was a very popular item in 1620, during the reign of Louis XIII. Another was early American, of a type favored by Thomas Jefferson. Those in the trade call it an Esopus Spitzenberg. This is only the beginning of my acquisitions. I plan to get more soon. For example, I have my eye on a nice Edward VII, and when I get it, I'm going to do just what I did with the first two. I'm going to eat it.

It's O.K. They're apples. Louis XIII didn't sit on his Calville Blancs, he had them for dessert. The Esopus Spitzenberg, a fruit of agrarian democracy, was Thomas Jefferson's favorite apple. Every time I bite into one I imagine myself writing the Declaration of Independence. I also pen a note to King George III to go along with his copy: "Dear King, How do you like them apples?"

The Edward VII is another old-fashioned apple, what the purveyors call an antique, although apples aren't antiques the way desks and chairs are. Individual apples are grown right now, in our own time—the present. It's the varieties that are old. And, like old furniture, they're disappearing. The same is true of many old varieties of vegetables, like the famed Jenny Lind muskmelon—as far as I know the

129

only vegetable ever to have been eulogized in the pages of
The Wall Street Journal. It must have been good.

I ordered the apples so that I don't have to read their
obituaries, too. Once I decide which ones I like, I'm going
to order trees and grow my own, right next to the garden
with the heirloom vegetables (that's what the old-time varieties like the Jenny Lind are called). For the spring I'm
thinking of Low's Champion shell beans, Rocky Ford honey-
dews, Pike rutabagas, and that good old-fashioned, non-
hybrid, open-pollinated Golden Bantam sweet corn.

I'm not alone. This is a trend. I know because everything
I do is part of a trend. I was born in 1949, which was, in
itself, trendy. In the sixties I had long hair and went on
peace marches. Later, while still young, I moved to an urban
area and became a professional (sort of). It's demographic
destiny; if I'm starting to buy old-time apples and heirloom
rutabaga seeds, the whole culture is on the edge of, or perhaps already in, the era of the biological antique. The passion for old objects is about to reach, in my generation, its
ultimate form. Forget chairs and tables, porcelain and silver. We've combined our taste for old furniture with our
love for herbal tea and hiking clothes, and we're going after
the *natural* past. We want the old genetic furniture from
the planet's attic (the good pieces, of course). "Give us that
old-time tomato" is our hymn, and you can bet there's somebody ready to sell it to us, with a kilo of amaranth on the
side.

Even the government is involved. It has a National Seed
Storage Laboratory, where more than 200,000 varieties of
seed are preserved in a kind of giant Burpee's Memorial
Garden Museum. (The lab, coincidentally, is located in Fort
Collins, Colorado, the home of the famous, but elusive, micro
pig.) Home gardeners do something similar through the
Seed Savers Exchange, growing and preserving seeds from
disappearing cultivars. And there are commercial opera-

tions as well. As with all the other things my generation loves, antique fruits and vegetables have inspired mail-order catalogues. These fairly throb with historical romance. My favorite is from Southmeadow Fruit Gardens of Lakeside, Michigan, which carries the Lady Apple, "known in Europe as Api or Pomme d'Api . . . Some writers even trace its origin to Appius Claudius, the Roman censor who constructed the Appian Way and who is asserted to have brought the apple from Peloponnesus." From the Peloponnesus—can you imagine?

My vegetable seed catalogue, from Johnny's Selected Seeds, of Albion, Maine, is more restrained. But the name of the town does suggest, if not Arcadia, at least pre-Thatcher Britain, and the text hints at an unspoiled American past. Rhode Island White Cap, for instance, is described as "an authentic, 8-rowed white flint corn of the Narragansett Indians." This is a good thing to have around in the era of monoculture. Because so many farmers plant the same varieties now, their crops are more susceptible to disease. The 1970 corn blight wiped out a fifth of the nation's corn crop, but I'll bet it didn't hit Rhode Island White Cap. Presumably, by growing it, I can kill two birds with one stone ground cornmeal muffin. I preserve genetic diversity, and I get to pretend I'm a Narragansett Indian in pre-Columbian America. Of course it doesn't pay to think too hard about what happened to the genome of the Narragansetts themselves.

Such are the pleasures of biological nostalgia, pleasures that I should point out are distinct from those of the scientific discipline closest to antique collecting—paleontology. It might seem that paleontologists go after the real biological antiques, and it's true that their subject is the history of life. But they only collect remnants. Usually you can't eat what they find. And the nature of their lust for the past is fundamentally different from the urges that send

a person in search of Ashmead's Kernel (a great old russet
apple that I got from Southmeadow Fruit Gardens). Paleontologists do not want to live in the past. They just want
to learn about it, and what they've learned is that it wasn't
so great. There was one mass extinction after another, com-
ets kept falling, there was always some new predator evolv-
ing, volcanoes were a constant danger, and there were these
godawful spasms of orogeny. (I think talk like this is why
geology has become so popular recently. It's sex without
guilt—in fact, without sex.) The rest of us aren't so clear-
headed. We seek out things from the past because we don't
like a present in which supermarket tomatoes are designed
to survive global thermonuclear war and we're not.

Nowhere is the underlying nature of biological nostalgia
clearer than in the popular fascination with the ice ages.
This doesn't have to do with collecting antique animals,
exactly; that's very hard to do. It has to do with antique
varieties of people. Ice Age Person is very popular right
now. In addition to movies and books (*Iceman* and *The Clan
of the Cave Bear*), there was a recent exhibit of ice age art
at the American Museum of Natural History in New York
called, romantically, "Dark Caves, Bright Visions." It had
lots of great jewelry, art that I could understand, and I
learned from it that these people not only had furs, they
had designers. As the book based on the exhibit puts
it, "Several of the 110 or so engravings of humans from
the 15,000-year-old Magdalenian site of La Marche in
France . . . seem fully dressed in tailored clothing with cuffs
and collars." The fall line for 13,000 B.C.

I think the exhibit offered reason enough to yearn for
Magdalenian times. There were lots of big mammals to
spear, low population density, Sundays in the cave with
Giorg. But somebody always has to come up with a new,
improved version. *Newsweek* did a cover article on the ice
ages. It ran a picture of Ice Age Man. He was Don Johnson.

He didn't have his T-shirt on, but I recognized him anyway. He had the right amount of beard, and he was displaying his trademark dullard's pout. There was even a young woman in lynx, or maybe fox, holding on to his arm and leaning her head on his shoulder in what looked (to the layman) suspiciously like a 1950s romantic stupor.

I would consider this an isolated incident of wishful paleoanthropology except that the woman looked as if she might be related to Daryl Hannah, who starred in *The Clan of the Cave Bear*. You may recall her as the debutante raised by Neanderthals. As an actress, Hannah seems to specialize in the extreme boundaries of the human species; in other movies she has played the roles of mermaid and performance artist. I like Daryl Hannah, even if the Neanderthals didn't. (They thought she was incredibly ugly, which is probably why they went extinct.) But like her or not, I have to say she didn't belong in *The Clan of the Cave Bear*. It makes the death curse of the Mog-ur so much less scary when the foremost question in your mind is not whether Ayla will survive, but how she kept her skin so soft and white.

I don't doubt that life in the ice ages was great, probably better than in the 1950s, which I remember as one long effort not to get beaten up. But I'll bet my totem (House Mouse) that there was nobody in the paleolithic with Daryl Hannah's complexion. I know who was there. I've seen those sculptures of Ice Age Woman. You know the ones I mean— the *big* ones. I know all about the eye of the beholder, but I think few modern beholders would be prepared to date the Venus of Willendorf. As for the men, they were human, but they didn't look like Don Johnson; they looked like George Shultz.

I say we stick to fruits and vegetables. They really did taste better in the old days. And if we want to pursue a real golden age, there's no better way to do it than with apples.

We could go back before the ice ages; we could go *all* the way back, to the time when nobody had to work, nobody had any clothes, and there was no original sin. Why not? Why not go after the ultimate biological antique, the original apple? That's what I really want growing in my yard. I can taste it already, sweeter than a Delicious, prettier than a Pomme d'Api, crisper than a Calville Blanc, big, russet, richly flavored, and forbidden, the favorite apple not of Thomas Jefferson but of God.

Science "Я" Us

I now have in my house two microscopes, a chemistry set, a geology lab, a gyroscope, Uncle Milton's Giant Ant Farm, and a bunch of dead Sea Monkeys in a Micro-Vue Ocean Zoo. I acquired this technical and zoological menagerie because of a flaw in my character. I'm an evangelical consumer. This doesn't mean I buy a lot of Bibles. It means that I believe in salvation through shopping. Like most religious beliefs, this one isn't rational. In actuality, I'm continually disappointed. Nothing, not even the new Walkman or the pre-abused blue jeans, has brought quite the happiness I hoped for. But then, not everybody gets cured at Lourdes either.

My last shopping episode, one might almost call it a seizure, occurred just before last Christmas. I was in Toys "Я" Us buying gifts in my usual way—one for them, one for me. I turned down the science toys aisle and there before me stood shelves brimming with faux chrome microscopes, plastic models of the human skull (always big at Yuletide), chemistry sets that promised hundreds and thousands of experiments. "Scientific Fun," the print on the packages blared, and "Research Set," and—my favorite—"Here AT LAST is the Miracle of Nature That Goes BEYOND The WILDEST DREAMS OF SCIENCE." Suddenly the fluores-

135

cent light seemed to acquire a revelatory luminescence, the kind of blinding glare that would have struck Paul if it had been the subway he took to Damascus. There it was, all boxed up for me, the joy and struggle of intellectual pursuit. I had heard that you couldn't buy happiness, but nobody had ever told me you couldn't buy science. I bought it, and I took it home.

Then I opened it up. The awful thing about gifts is that you never really get what you want, even if you buy them for yourself. With the first few scientific disciplines I suffered grave disappointments. Gyroscopy, for example, turned out to be kind of limited. Once you've balanced the thing on top of a pencil, you've pretty much plumbed the depths of excitement in that field. Geology wasn't much better. In fact, the geology research kit I bought, for $19.97, was considerably less interesting than the gyroscope. This isn't what John McPhee had led me to believe. John McPhee is a writer who treats geology as if it were something incredibly interesting, like Cajun food. He writes about basins and ranges, mountain building, plate tectonics, and volcanoes. He reported what I consider to be the only interesting thing ever said about golf, which is that golf courses are human attempts to reproduce the glaciated terrain of Scotland—where the game began.

There was nothing this interesting in my research set. What I had paid $20 for was a collection of twenty-four pieces of rock, most of them fairly mousy (slate, sandstone, lava, and of course the ever popular Piedmontite schist), a magnifying glass, and a seven-page booklet. My guess is that it wasn't written by McPhee. I quote, "No. 6 Gabbro (plutonic rock). Consisting mainly of pyroxene and feldspar rich in calcium, it is a black rock with rough grains." I guess this is what makes kids love science.

I turned from rocks to raisins. In my chemistry kit I

discovered an experiment that I call the "Lazarus Raisin." This is what you do: drop a raisin into a glass of seltzer or soda and tell the raisin to go up and down. I did this with my kids. I said, with feeling: "Rise up, raisin!" and "Go down, raisin!" as the raisin rose and fell, borne by seltzer bubbles. My two-year-old got into the spirit of this. She raised her arms and shouted like a faith healer when the raisin lay too long, apparently paralyzed, at the bottom of the glass of seltzer. "Rise up raisin! Rise up raisin! Rise up raisin!" she called out in her best basso profundo, stamping her feet, stretching her hands to heaven, or perhaps to the ceiling. Unfortunately, she always got bored before the raisin got cured, so she never saw the actual miracle take place.

Obviously, we had hit upon the perfect Bible Belt soda commercial. But something was missing. I wasn't experiencing what Einstein experienced when he thought up general relativity. At least I hope I wasn't. Shouting at the raisin didn't have the feeling I was looking for. It didn't feel like the search for the structure of DNA. It felt more like a new feature on the David Letterman show—stupid food tricks. I suppose I could have gone on. I could have made borax crystals. I could have put lemon juice in milk so that it curdled and produced casein. I could have used the casein to make paint. I could have painted something. My heart wasn't in it.

My heart, if truth be told, is and always has been in ethology. I've always longed to be out in the field, observing African elephants, or spending a year with the giant river otters of Brazil. The animal world is so rich, the discoveries so varied and intriguing. I still recall my astonishment at learning that when two related elephants meet each other after an absence of weeks or months, they sometimes charge together and enter into a kind of ecstatic embrace, which makes them both so excited they tend to urinate and defecate in the process of saying hello. When I first read about this it confirmed my belief that it's neither language nor intelligence but manners that set human beings apart from animals.

Unfortunately, I've never been able to get the funding to go to Africa or South America. I did, however, have the $6.97 I needed to buy the "Miracle of Nature That Goes BEYOND etc., etc." Beware the inexpensive miracle. In this case the miracle is, or are, sea monkeys, which also go under the less transcendental name of, yes, Virginia, brine shrimp. Of course these are bigger than average brine shrimp and they're supposed to live longer, too. It seemed reasonable to assume they might make an appropriate subject for a household ethologist. And perhaps someone whose animals lived to participate in the Super Sea Monkey Race or the forthcoming Sea Monkey baseball would have more to report on in the way of behavior. (Both of these activities take advantage of the classic brine shrimp tendency to swim upstream.) Mine lived their short lives without the pleasures of sport, as far as I could see. They hatched all right. And they took up swimming around their container, little dots with the pale color of blind cave catfish. They didn't look like pets to me. They looked more like intestinal parasites, the sort of things you might find wriggling around in a glass of the Nile River. Despite my best efforts, they lived only a week, and in all honesty I can't say I was sorry when they died.

I would never say that about *Pogonomyrmex californicus*. These are my ants—the ones in Uncle Milton's Giant Ant Farm. These are the creatures that finally provided some behavior for me to study. You can't go wrong with ants. Whether you've got them in a homemade formicarium or in Uncle Milton's farm, with the little silo and windmill, they're still insects of distinction. For example, ants are the source of the single most problematic word in the English language: "formication." It means "an abnormal sensation resembling that made by insects creeping in or on the skin." Dermatologists learning English as a second language face the gravest difficulties, but because of the obvious perils, this word is seldom taught even to those learning English as a first language. Instead we learn the colloquial "creeps," as in "he gives me the creeps."

So few creatures are wonders of etymology *and* entomology. Ants are tops. Or, as E. O. Wilson of Harvard, a major figure in formic science, says, "Ants are in every sense of the word the dominant social insects." Besides which, you can get them through the mail. I've been watching my ants now for a couple of weeks, and the thing I like best about them is that they're still alive. They're digging tunnels, and making hills around the silly little silo. They're eating and bustling about. They work; I watch. And I've made a couple of discoveries, one of which is that they don't know how to swim. I put too much water in the farm one day and it made a little puddle. I watched, stunned, as one of my *Pogonomyrmex* tried to walk over the water, stumbled, and fell in head first. I thought it was drowning. I was going to save it until I remembered it was an ant. I'm fairly sure that ants don't breathe through their mouths, and while I was thinking about exactly how they do breathe, this one managed to save itself.

Another notable thing about ants is that they don't panic when something awful happens to them. I say this not only because of the drowning false alarm (there was a bit of agitated feeler-waving in that incident) but because of something I witnessed in the graveyard detail. When the ants aren't digging or eating, they're carrying dead ants, or parts of dead ants, off to some nether corner of Uncle

Milton's farm.* I worry a lot about this, given the plague that struck my sea monkeys. But I've been impressed by their seriousness. Several ants were, shall we say, bruised, as I transferred them from the shipping vial to the farm. One of these ended up without the back half of its body. I saw this ant, insouciant, carrying a piece of a dead comrade, or perhaps of itself, off to the dump. This is the kind of animal that Vince Lombardi would have loved.

I'd like to end this piece on a happy note, with me in front of Uncle Milton's Giant Ant Farm pursuing my ethological studies, happy, for once, with my purchases. However, as the days passed an ethical crisis arose. Did I mention the microscopes? I bought one that looked like chrome and was supposed to go up to $1200\times$, with slides, tweezers, and prepared slides, for $42.97. When I tried it out, everything at every power was just a rainbow pattern, the kind of kaleidoscopic image people liked to look at in the '60s when they were smoking marijuana. It was a terrible disappointment. The pollen, the cat hair, the bumblebee leg—they all looked alike.

I ordered a better, more expensive microscope. This one only went up to $300\times$, and it didn't have any kit, but it cost a hundred dollars. It took a very long time to come. Finally, it arrived, on December 24. It was beautiful, made out of metal instead of plastic, with achromatic correction to keep the rainbows away, and its own wooden case. And it worked beautifully. I tried all the prepared slides that had come with the other kit. The sunflower pollen looked like little burrs, and the tulip pollen like chips of semi-

*His full name is Milton Levine and he incorporated, as Uncle Milton, Inc., in 1954. He started selling his ant farm on July 4, 1956, and has sold, up to now, about 8 million. Most of them are pretty good, but the one I had as a child never worked for reasons that have always puzzled me. Recent conversations with my parents revealed to me that we may, in fact, have never sent away for the ants. That would do it.

precious stones. The bumblebee leg with its pink stain was wonderfully clear, and hairy. What to look at next? Well, if a bumblebee leg was fascinating, a *Pogonomyrmex* leg would be too, wouldn't it? Or perhaps a whole *Pogonomyrmex*.

I was beset by conflicting voices. One asked me whether I was an ethologist, with respect for my subjects as individual creatures, or a reductionist—I mean this literally, in the sense of reducing a *Pogonomyrmex* to legs, thorax, and abdomen. Jane Goodall wouldn't dissect her chimps, after all. The other voice asked me if I was an idiot. It pointed out to me that we weren't talking about primates. We weren't talking about mammals. We were talking about a creature that didn't notice when half of its body was gone. It also pointed out to me that, according to E. O. Wilson, "at any given moment there are at least 10^{15} [in layman's terms, a zillion] living ants on the earth." It didn't know whether this included half-ants.

I don't know either. But I blame what happened on shopping. As long as I had had only the rotten microscope, the ants were safe. What was there to see? But I had to have a new, better, more expensive microscope. And as any scientist knows, once you've got the instrument, you've got to use it. (I consider what happened to me and the ants to be an excellent argument against nuclear weapons research.) The images were so clear with the new microscope. I couldn't help but imagine a *Pogonomyrmex* at $50\times$—the polished amber abdomen, the intricate mouthparts, the delicately furred feelers, the faceted ebony eyes. I don't want to go into the whole sad story. Suffice it to say that the reality went BEYOND My WILDEST DREAMS, and there were $10^{15} - 1$ living ants on earth last Christmas day.

A Gastronomer
in Paris

*The discovery of a new dish does more for human happiness
than the discovery of a star.*

—Jean Anthelme Brillat-Savarin

T rue wisdom doesn't fade. That observation was made
in 1825 in Brillat-Savarin's brilliant *The Physiology
of Taste,* a book that I might point out was published
more than a quarter-century before Darwin's *Origin of
Species.* And it's as valid today as it was then. Not that
either I or Brillat-Savarin has anything against astronomy.
The point was merely to beef up another noble science,
gastronomy, and to give comfort to its practitioners, the
gastronomers.*

Brillat-Savarin's work would be, and in fact is, a classic
in any field. It's a book of meditations in which he treats,
with equal seriousness, the "Theory of Frying," "The Origin
of Sciences," "The Pullet of Bresse," and "The End of the

---

*You may find, in food magazines, that the term "gastronome" has
been lifted, undigested, from the French. If we had an Académie Amér-
icaine to defend our language and culture, I'm sure they would object.
After all, is Carl Sagan an astronome?

World." This is as it should be. Brillat-Savarin's only mistake was in thinking that the world would recognize, as he had, the supreme importance of good food. He foresaw a great academy of gastronomy, on the order of the Sorbonne, or Harvard, or Berlitz, which would make the name of its founder famous. "It [the name] will be repeated from century to century with those of Noah, of Bacchus, of Triptolemus . . ." Ah yes, Triptolemus.*

It should be obvious that Brillat-Savarin was French. Here, after all, is a man who devoted his life not only to eating, but also to *thinking* about eating. Only a Frenchman would enumerate the four, and only four, classes of people who eat, God forgive them, bouilli (beef that has been simmered to make stock, or bouillon). Only a Frenchman could say, "Fish, by which I indicate all species of it considered as a whole, is for a philosopher an endless source of meditation and astonishment."†

Of course that's what the French are for, isn't it? That's why we have them, to produce great food, and a certain sort of exotic genius. They, their cuisine, and even their insufferable self-importance are a kind of international resource. Or so I like to think. To be fair, I would have to admit that this image of the French is a stereotype like any other. And I would have to say also that this stereotype is being promulgated by a man who has spent more time in Madawaska, Maine, than he has in Paris. (This isn't as bad as it sounds; Madawaska, although it doesn't have the Louvre,

*The goddess Demeter taught Triptolemus the arts of agriculture, which he spread throughout Greece.
†In reading Brillat-Savarin, I relied on the translation of M. F. K. Fisher, whose notes seem to me every bit as good as the text. She says in her footnote to the fish comment, which I reproduce here in part (in my fish footnote), "The most meditative statement I have ever read about Fish, not a fish or the fish but Fish, is a poem from the Japanese." It is: "Young leaves ev'rywhere/ The mountain cuckoo singing;/ My first Bonito!"

is mostly French. Its people are the Acadians of Longfellow's *Evangeline*, who, transplanted to Louisiana, became Cajuns.)

You can see that I'm deeply involved with the French, although largely in my mind. Probably the best way to put my relationship with them is to say, as Woody Allen did about a blind date (he's lucky he wasn't involved with a Frenchwoman), "I *really* have mixed feelings about [them]." I know that not everyone shares these feelings. Some people just plain don't like the French. No doubt these people are all Class 3 Bouilli-Eaters: "The uninterested, who not having received the sacred fire from heaven, look on meals as a duty to be performed." But for those of us who have a taste for culinary art (and paintings of water lilies—between meals) the French are, well, they are to us what "Fish" is to a philosopher—an endless source of meditation and astonishment.

That said, it should be clear why it depressed me to receive in the mail my issues of FAST. The acronym stands for French Advances in Science and Technology. FAST is a newsletter, sent out by the French embassy, to provide "information to Americans on the achievements of France in high technology." Sad enough to see the French abasing (from the Middle French *abaisser*) themselves in front of Anglophones in such an unsubtle and shameless fashion. What do they care what Americans think? But even worse are the headlines "Wide Band Switching," "Cat Leukemia Vaccine" and "Robot Trains Come to O'Hare"—this from the country of Proust.

The French are inventing dental prostheses and new machines for kidney stone therapy; they make smart cards, the Concorde, the Ariane satellite launcher, and the Exocet missiles that were such a hit in the Falklands. They're taking their place in international high technology, and in the process they're ruining one of my favorite theories of eternal life. In this theory, which I don't think is associated with any established religion (I heard it not in a church but in a bar), the dead not only rise again but they keep their nationalities. The difference between heaven and hell is in the jobs the different national groups are assigned. In heaven, the English are the police, the Germans the engineers, and the French the cooks. In hell, the English are the cooks, the French the engineers, and the Germans the police.

FAST also reported that the French had recently built a new $500 million Science and Industry Museum at La Villette in northeast Paris. Here, in one location, was a chance to see what science had really done to the French, and vice versa. I've never shied from duty. In this I hold with Mother Teresa. I saw her on television the other day and she said that we should accept God's will. Took the words right out of my mouth. She said, to be precise, that if He wants you poor and on the street, take it with a smile. If He wants you in a palace, that's O.K. too, as long as He puts you there and you don't put yourself there. Well, He doesn't speak to me directly, at least not in English, but I got the point. He wanted me in Paris.

Since this is a science magazine I won't talk about the salmon tartare, the wild duck grilled over a wood fire, the stew of wild boar, the *tarte Tatin,* the chocolate mousse dusted with cinnamon, or the Volnay that was ordered so that its hint of raspberry would complement a peppery breast of duck, but which also seemed to go quite well with the venison. Let's just say that a country that can cook like that has no business spending its time on cat leukemia. And a man who has the chance to eat like that has no business using up valuable meal time at a science museum. You only live once, and when you die, you have no idea who the cooks will be.

There was, however, the issue of how Mother Teresa, and

the IRS, would view my trip if I didn't go to the science museum. I went, sacrificing my chance to go with my family to a place that makes its hot chocolate by melting chocolate bars. I heard later that the resulting liquid was so thick it began to harden in the cup if you dawdled. One member of my family complained that it was so rich he could only drink two cups. As for my meal at the museum, I had a pasty *pâté de foie gras* spread on cold toast. Worse yet, at one snack bar the *café express,* thick and black, was served in plastic cups. An equivalent break with American tradition would be to hawk draft beer at Yankee Stadium in teeny china demitasses. At least the wine was served in glass glasses, and, to my satisfaction, cost less than a cup of orange soda.

There were also exhibits, some of them excellent. I particularly liked the fish hatchery, which I took to be about the history and philosophy of cooking, taking trout *meunière* beyond proximate causes to its ultimate origins. There was a display of hydroponics, where salad was being grown. And this theme was picked up in a space station display. At this exhibit, a voice reminiscent of Brillat-Savarin spoke to anyone who had rented headphones. It explained how certain metal alloys could be made in weightless space and not on earth. On earth, it said, because the molten metals are of different densities, they would separate, "rather like an Italian salad dressing, in which the oil always comes to the top." Gastronomy was not dead.

"The Plastic Years," as the exhibit was called, reminded me of another national talent—for couture. The heat-retaining qualities of certain plastics were suggested by a mannequin standing on a pedestal. She was holding ski poles and had on bright red plastic ski boots, a white knit cap, a red bikini bottom but no top, and a transparent plastic coat and pants. The point here was that this outfit, of some kind of polyethylene, reflected the *infrarouge* while being

95 percent transparent to the ultraviolet—or tanning—rays. Not only that, but you could see right through it. The material hadn't been developed for semi-nude skiing, however, but for agriculture. You see, "this film permits to realize very performing greenhouses." (It's a good thing I'm bilingual.)

By the time I'd seen the skiing mannequin, I was beginning to warm to the idea of the French being involved in science, or at least in science museums. Perhaps technology was only a spice that brought out the essential flavor of the French character, like thyme on a perfectly cooked rack of lamb. It was thus in a generous, Francophilic frame of mind that I entered "Odorama."

As the name may or may not suggest, the purpose of Odorama was to demonstrate communication through smell. I passed through double doors, designed to seal in odors, and found myself in a small, dimly lit chamber with a lot of French people. On one wall was a screen and a panel to allow viewers, who in this case were also smellers, to select short film segments. First we watched children trying to burn a fox out of its den. When they lit the brand, we smelled fire. When the camera brought us inside the fox den—we smelled that. Next, a boy put bubble gum in his mouth and proceeded to walk to a barn with a friend. We experienced, in turn, the intense and unmistakable smells of bubble gum, hay (or maybe straw; I guess it wasn't that unmistakable), and cow manure.

The next bit of film was of another order altogether. It was from the movie *Swann in Love,* with Jeremy Irons. I want to warn parents who may pass this book on to their children, or borrow it from them, that this is a *French* museum we're talking about, and that *love,* in France, always seems to involve some kind of sex. Now, if you're willing to go on, place yourself, with me, in Odorama, and watch the screen:

Jeremy Irons, as Swann, is sitting alone in an elegant horse-drawn carriage, with an air of melancholy. A memory of another carriage ride thrusts itself into his consciousness. He's in the same carriage, but not alone. Next to him is a lovely woman dressed in an elegant gown with a precipitous and alluring décolletage. The allure has its effect on Swann as well as us. He's drawn to an orchid corsage anchored at the midpoint of the neckline. Gazing into the woman's eyes, he tucks the orchid into the gown. Then he bows his head to the orchid and inhales deeply. Then he gets a bit carried away—with style, to be sure, as befits a French gentleman. But soon enough the gown slips, as I've always suspected such gowns were wont to do, and it's no longer the orchid, but his lover's unclothed, unrestrained breasts (with the orchid in there somewhere) that Swann is kissing and ca-ressing with abandon.

Meanwhile, back in Odorama, every man in the room is leaning toward the screen, inhaling deeply. I'm surprised we all didn't hyperventilate. Eventually the aroma of the orchid filled the room, Swann's recollection, and the film clip, ended, and we all straightened up, exhaling now, with sighs, as we realized that not only was this just a memory, it wasn't even our memory.

I'd always felt that passion was lacking from science, particularly from the average museum of science and in-dustry. And yet here it was in Odorama, in full flower. What could one say, except perhaps *Vive la France*? Certainly, this was conclusive proof that my fear for the French had been misplaced. When it came to muting the French char-acter, technology never had a chance. Indeed, I think people will soon be talking about French science with the same kind of interest and appreciation that used to be reserved for French postcards.

You see, we do need the French. In this country scientists may do research on smell and memory and sexual desire, but you would need a Ph.D. to figure out that any of this had anything to do with the sort of feelings that might make you try to inhale a movie screen in a public place. For that you need the French, because you're not going to get this version of Odorama in St. Paul, Minnesota, although there's a great science museum there. I don't think it will play in New York, either, at the American Museum of Natural History, or in Washington, D.C., at the Smithsonian. Kids go to these places, American kids. And in America we don't show heavy petting to kids, not in a museum, not with characters from Proust. We say, as Marie Antionette wouldn't have said: Let them look at minerals and gems. Later, when they're older, when they're ready, they can go to Paris— for the food, and the art, and the science.

The Fear of Cod

Two stories:

Somewhere in Oregon, young salmon are swimming in a Plexiglas corral set within a larger tank. The larger tank is filled with ling cod that are constantly slamming their noses against the walls of the corral in a desperate attempt to eat the salmon. The point is to train the salmon to be afraid. I'm sure it works. If I were an itty bitty fish and the giant maw of death kept crashing into Plexiglas an inch away from me, I would be even more fearful than I am now, as a full-sized human being, which is pretty fearful considering that there are no giant fish trying to eat me . . . most of the time.

Meanwhile, A. M. Rosenthal, former executive editor of *The New York Times,* the most powerful newspaper in the country, if not the world, is visiting the Galápagos Archipelago. He discovers that the marine iguanas, sea lions, and birds aren't scared of him. Presumably, it's all but inconceivable for the former executive editor of *The New York Times* to encounter a creature he doesn't frighten. Rosenthal is surprised and charmed, and reports the experience in an Op Ed page column he now writes, along with his conclusion that the absence of predation (what we in jour-

nalism call "editing") has allowed these creatures to exist
in some ideal, pristine condition. He writes, "The absence
of fear is the best and the original state, a thought to hug."

I call this the Huggums* hypothesis, and I put it together
with the salmon story because each, in its way, suggests a
meditation about fear, albeit different meditations.

First, Huggums:

The islands that inspired Rosenthal were discovered in
1535 by Spaniards and shortly thereafter became a prime
destination for nature cruises. First it was the H.M.S. *Beagle,* then the American Museum of Natural History and
Inca Floats vacations. Everybody who goes to Galápagos
writes about them—Darwin, Annie Dillard, Kurt Vonne-
gut, Rosenthal, Irenaus Eibl-Eibesfeldt (I'll get to him later).
Many of these writers have noted an absence of fear in some
of the animals.

Darwin, for instance, found the birds quite tame, but the
iguanas were afraid of him and ran away and hid in crev-
ices. No wonder, considering the sort of things Darwin did
to lizards. In *The Voyage of the Beagle* he writes, with no
sense of shame that I can see, about how he confirmed that
these animals, though adapted to the water, still clung for
safety to the land: "I threw one several times as far as I
could, into a deep pool left by the returning tide; but it
invariably returned in a direct line to the spot where I
stood." Darwin continues, "Perhaps this singular piece of
apparent stupidity may be accounted for by the circumstance that this reptile has no enemy whatever on shore,
whereas at sea it must often fall a prey to the numerous
sharks." In other words, the iguanas were saying to them-

---

*Huggums is the name of a very cute doll, which really is worth
hugging, and bears no relationship to any theory about fear, real or
imagined.

selves: This guy Darwin may throw me around a bit but the sharks are going to *kill* me.

There are other indications that the idyl Rosenthal saw is really a kind of show put on for the tourists, that beneath the Edenlike surface lies the sad squalor of island animal life. The boobies, in particular, suffer tremendously. They're always being mugged by the frigate birds, as Eibl-Eibesfeldt documented in his book *Galápagos*. As soon as a booby got a fish, "the hovering, alert frigate birds, which had been keeping a watch on the booby, would swoop down on him and jab their beaks into his back and head." Eibl-Eibesfeldt also observed territorial posturing and ritual battles for turf and females among both sea lions and iguanas.

Of course it's possible the boobies experienced not fear but only annoyance when they were assaulted and robbed of their dinners. In any case, we can't dispute the fact that whatever else they fear, the sea lions, iguanas, and birds weren't afraid of Rosenthal. And that's enough to evince in him feelings of peace and good will. However, the Huggums hypothesis, as I read it, goes deeper. Its fundamental point seems to be that lack of fear is the "original" state. Rosenthal talks about this lack of fear being "what was meant to be." Before I explain why I think this is complete nonsense, I want to emphasize that I am no more of a scientist than Rosenthal is. In this sense we're both iguanas who may be picked up by our tails and flung out to sea by some biologist who really knows what he's talking about. What's more, Rosenthal is the dominant iguana. Still, if you don't challenge these guys once in a while you never get any females.

The only original state I can think of where fear was absent is Eden. There, it's true, the lion didn't eat the lamb. But let's be frank. Recent studies of the diet of lions have shown that as a non-miracle-based ecosystem, the Garden of Eden doesn't work. On the planet earth, for which we have better data, the situation is different. It seems pretty likely that the origin of fear has something to do with this business of getting eaten. And, in the history of life, things started eating other things almost as soon as there was anything worth eating. True, the blue-green algae weren't munched on for a billion or so years, and I would go so far as to say they never experienced fear. But they never experienced anything. By the time consciousness emerged, by the time it was possible for an organism to be aware of its environment, the world was already rife with predators, and with the fear they tend to evoke. In other words, there was no Eden, fear-wise. For most of us (poisonous caterpillars excepted for a variety of reasons) life is, always has been, and is *meant* to be scary.

I do have some actual scientific support for this idea. This is where the salmon come in. I talked to the head fish-frightener, Bori Olla, a professor of oceanography at Oregon State University's Hatfield Marine Science Center. Though it's hard for me to believe, Olla came to study salmon even though he isn't a fly fisherman. He got involved with them because he wondered how a young fish raised in a hatchery, where there's neither joy nor fear, would cope when it was released into the ocean, a place full of all sorts of emotions. (Remember the "oceanic" feeling.)

This is my phrasing. What Olla actually said was that a hatchery is a "deprived" environment, and the fish that come out of it are "naïve." He considered that these fish would face (as do all living things) two fundamental tasks in their struggle to survive—eating and not being eaten. If they couldn't catch prey they would starve, and if they were eaten . . . well, there's no need to finish that sentence. Olla wanted to know how naïveté would affect the salmon's ability to accomplish these tasks. He discovered at the outset that no matter how naïve a fish was, it quickly learned to recognize shrimp and smaller fish as food and to catch them. Avoiding being eaten turned out to be more of a problem.

First, Olla put twenty or thirty small salmon in a big tank with a ling cod, a voracious, not at all naïve predator. If these hatchery salmon were Mary Poppins, the ling cod was Mack the Knife. It went right to work and within an hour it ate half the salmon. The survivors, after having had a few lay days, were put back in the tank with the ling cod once again. They now fared much better than their naïve conspecifics. But it wasn't clear why. One possibility was that they were faster, quicker, and smarter to begin with, and that's why they survived the first time. Another was that they had learned something, namely that if there was one thing in life they should do to keep on living it was to stay the hell away from ling cod.

To see if the training had had an effect apart from cod-induced survival of the fittest, Olla introduced the corral, the Plexiglas barrier in which young salmon could be frightened but not eaten. Olla tried, in other words, to put "the fear of cod" into them.* It worked, not as well as being right in the tank with the predator, but it worked. When they faced the ling cod, trained salmon fared better than naïve salmon.

You could take this as simple confirmation of what Rosenthal was talking about. These salmon existed in a kind of dull idyl in the hatchery, and learned to be afraid when there was something to be afraid of. But Olla thinks the fish didn't actually learn fear, in the way a dog might learn not to do stuff on the rug that would get it pummeled with a rolled-up newspaper, but that the appearance of the ling cod awakened in the salmon a basic, genetic, life-enhancing capacity for complete and utter terror. Olla said that when

---

*This pun is the work of Ed Curtin of the department of information at Oregon State University.

hatchery fish are released into a natural environment, they seem at first unaware, dull, lacking a sense of themselves and the world around them. They're missing not only fear, but also territorial sense and other capacities that make a fish a fish. One might almost say they're not fully alive, that, in a fundamental way that has to do with their very identity, they're asleep. The ling cod wakes them right up.

And this is the real point. Fear is a part of being alive, a part of who we are, whether we're salmon or people. It isn't some sad addition to what used to be a pleasant existence. Some people even seek it out by riding roller coasters, rock climbing, spelunking, and hang-gliding. They're not grabbing gusto, they're grabbing fear. And the reason is that they don't want to feel that they're living in a hatchery. I guess I'm one of the lucky ones. I've never needed artificial stimulation to be frightened out of my wits. I experience a lot of fear just sitting at my desk. The list of things I'm afraid of (giant fish, A. M. Rosenthal, fear itself) is incredibly long, and what I take this to mean is that I'm living life to its fullest, every minute of every day.

Playing Doctor

E arlier this week I killed three emergency room patients in the space of about fifteen minutes. I sent
two into respiratory arrest and one into cardiac arrest. (This is known among trauma interns as a hat trick.)
Of course it's possible that they didn't die. For all I know,
after I blew it some other doctor called a Code Blue or a
Code Purple (idiot in the emergency room) and saved Eugene Wilson, 21, motorcycle accident victim, or Donnie
Brooks, 20, the victim of a stabbing incident outside the
River Tavern, which, judging from Donnie's appearance before I let his heart stop, isn't the kind of place I'm ever going
for a drink or a stabbing incident.

I know this sounds bizarre, and the truth is there weren't
really three different patients. The truth is I killed Donnie
Brooks twice. I was able to do this for two reasons. First,
I'm not a doctor. Second, I did it on DxTer, a combination
of video and computer technology that's used to train medical students the way flight simulators help train pilots—
a kind of "St. Elsewhere" simulator.

DxTer is part of the current interaction bonanza. By interaction I don't mean conversation or psychotherapy or
being mugged—the classic forms of interaction. Those all
involve other people. The boom now is in interacting with

television of one sort or another, often for educational purposes. Usually this means you affect what's happening on the screen, although sometimes the screen affects you. For example, one company is making a set of remote-controlled robots for children's toys. The kid controls the good guys but the bad guys are controlled by inaudible signals from a television program on which they also appear. I suspect the show will also turn on your vacuum and drive your car if you don't watch out.

Moving up in age there's the interactive video courtroom at Harvard Law School, which allows students to act as counsel in a videotaped trial that appears on a computer monitor. The students use a computer keyboard to raise objections and cite precedents. The system is limited, of course. There's no provision for the force of oratory, or for bribes. There's also a law enforcement simulator. In one of this system's training dramas a life-sized woman on a large screen reaches into her pocketbook for either a driver's license or a gun. The law enforcer has to decide whether or not to blow her away. If he shoots, bullet holes appear on the screen and the action stops. I suppose this is what today's children think happens when you die. You're going along at regular speed in the movie of life, and the next thing you know—freeze frame! Or else you suffer a prolonged period of slow motion before the end.

The goal of all this educational interaction is to make better doctors, cops, and lawyers by letting them try out their knowledge in something more demanding than a written exam before we give them accident victims, live ammunition, and real money. I'm sure the simulators do what they're meant to, and that they'll all benefit society tremendously. But that isn't what interested me. What interested me was that all this was taking place on TV. Officially, it's video, on a computer monitor. But really, it's TV. It's happening on the same little screen that entranced us in childhood, the same screen that held me in thrall throughout my years of higher education, thus derailing my medical, legal, and law enforcement careers and forcing me to seek a less reputable form of employment. It's on the same screen on which I first saw "Sky King" (a flight simulator) and "Rawhide" (a masculinity simulator). It was on this screen that I watched "Gunsmoke," "Dragnet," "Maverick," "Perry Mason," "Dr. Kildare," and "Car 54, Where Are You?"

So when I read about the simulators I said to myself, Ooh! Ooh! Ooh! I got an idea! The idea, naturally, was to try out a video simulator, not because I wanted to learn to be a better doctor or cop, but because after years of watching TV shows I wanted to be *in* one.* The only question was which one. I didn't have much interest in lawyer shows. The law has never looked like a fun profession to me, except for the chance to hang out with Joyce Davenport. And while there was a certain appeal to the unrestrained violence of police dramas, as I understand it when the people on the cop simulator die, they don't bleed. On DxTer, they bleed.

Hospital drama definitely had the most appeal. It had great characters. I would be free to imagine myself as Ben Casey or Marcus Welby if I happened to be feeling grandiose, as the anxious and unpleasant Ehrlich on "St. Elsewhere" if I happened to be in a period of low self-esteem, or, most likely, as my all-time favorite television doctor, Hawkeye Pierce of the 4077th M*A*S*H. And in hospital shows, even if the characters are weak, or the plot fails to click, there's other interesting stuff—you know, blood gases, X-rays, ampicillin. The choice was clear.

---

*I'm sure all the people who use these things imagine themselves in TV or the movies. You can't tell me that rookie law enforcers, when the sergeant isn't around, don't give the dame with the pocketbook a crooked smile and say, just before they squeeze the trigger, "Go ahead, lady, make my day!"

I flew to San Diego to meet DxTer and talk to its creator, a doctor. His name is David Allan. He's the head of Intelligent Images, Inc. and he showed me the ropes on his brainchild, which is already in use in several medical schools and is being marketed by IBM. DxTer consists of a computer program, the computer itself, a video disc player, and a collection of video discs on which eight different cases are recorded, including stab wounds (Donnie Brooks), shotgun wounds (Victor Mercedes), chest trauma (Eugene Wilson), and diarrhea and vomiting (John Dircus). All are based on real medical cases and have been staged as short hospital dramas with actors and excellent special effects. This means that everything looks real. When you see Eugene Wilson gag and sputter while the trauma team intubates him (this involves thrusting what looks to be a plastic spout down his throat), it makes you incredibly glad you didn't get into medical school.

The cases, or episodes, are stored on video discs because a computer can immediately call up to a monitor any part of a disc; there's none of the rewinding and fast-forwarding required with tape. DxTer's computer program is the heart of the system. It determines what section of the video disc to show and tells the computer when to switch from the emergency room drama to a printed menu that offers various courses of action for the viewer to take. The screen is touch sensitive, so all you have to do is push "Examine" or "Diagnostics" or "Medicine/Therapeutics" to be offered a new list of possible medications or tests. All the arcana of medicine are at your fingertips. The program specifies a response to every possible decision a viewer can make, whether it's to flash images of the intubation the student has just ordered, or to suggest, politely, that when a man has uncontrollable diarrhea, it's no time to X-ray his foot.

I watched Allan whiz through the treatment of Eugene

Wilson once to pick up a few pointers before I took over. When I did, things happened all too fast, particularly for the patient.

Suddenly Eugene Wilson was wheeled into the emergency room, bleeding, bandaged, and wearing a pair of huge inflatable trousers to squeeze his legs and push the blood up into his thorax (do I sound like a doctor or what?). The paramedic said something like, "You think he's bad, you should've seen the bike." The head nurse looked at Eugene Wilson's shock pants and said, "Anything under the trousers?" I laughed. Nobody else did. Clearly this wasn't Korea.

The trauma team set to work on him. Then the screen switched to the menu, putting the victim in my hands. "Examine" was an obvious first choice. I pushed it and the team began to examine him. He wasn't in good shape. He reminded me of the old song, "There was blood on the saddle and blood on the ground, and a great big puddle of blood all around." I had him intubated (why not?), took a bunch of X-rays, and prescribed all the antibiotics I could get my hands on. DxTer implemented my orders. Occasionally DxTer acted on its own. It flashed the message, "The patient must be ventilated immediately," and then proceeded to have the team do it. At other times cryptic messages appeared on the screen, like "Capillary refill is delayed." What? I ordered a few more tests, some fluids, and tried to remember an episode of "M*A*S*H" that might help me. I was floundering; it was becoming obvious to me why people go to medical school.

The patient took a downhill turn. I ordered a consultant. He was on his way. I ordered a chaplain. Suddenly there was Eugene Wilson on the screen again, looking even worse. The nurse turned to me, and said, in what I thought was a rather accusatory tone, that the patient wasn't breathing. Why do you think I called the chaplain? I thought to myself.

Now I was starting to get irritated. I'd already cleared this guy's airway and intubated him. What was his problem? I decided to give him a proctoscopy. I figured that ought to wake him up. DxTer demurred. The proctoscopy wasn't indicated. The next thing I knew respiratory arrest ensued, I was booted out of the program and the emergency room, and DxTer suggested I try again. Well, if you ask me, if we'd given him the proctoscopy Eugene Wilson would be alive and walking around today, although perhaps not comfortably.

This wasn't the way the experts saw it. DxTer will give you an expert analysis of how you botched a case, if you ask for it. The experts claimed that Eugene Wilson had had a tension pneumothorax and that I should have put in a chest tube. Experts. They think they're so smart. I moved on to Donnie Brooks, to try my hand at stab wounds. The first time I neglected to clear his airway and he choked on his tongue, and the second time he didn't get enough fluids so he went into shock and his heart stopped. On that last try, I got a cost analysis of my work. The so-called experts may have saved Donnie Brooks, but they cost the hospital $1,852. I did much better. I got us out for under a grand—$842—not bad for a River Tavern knifing, I thought.

I certainly learned a few things from DxTer. I now know that if anybody at a party comes down with a tension pneumothorax, what you do is slap a chest tube into him. I learned what shock trousers are. I expect to see David Bowie or David Byrne—some David anyway—wearing them soon. And if I picked up this much, DxTer has got to be even more valuable to medical students, who actually know what a tension pneumothorax is, I hope.

DxTer isn't great TV, however. The thing is that as a doctor, I'm far less interesting, even to myself, than Alan Alda. And I realized as I dealt with the incessant demands of the patients—always bleeding, always needing fluids, or ventilation, or some tube or other—that I didn't need this grief. It wasn't my job. I've got problems of my own. And I get more than enough interaction in everyday life. What I want from television is a plot that just chugs along on its own, with no effort on my part. I want to watch the shows, not write them.

On the other hand, I'm all for the proliferation of training simulators for situations in which it's dangerous to jump right into the real thing, like marriage. There could be a marriage simulator with a choice of scenarios: Infidelity, Overdrawn Checkbook, Let's Talk About Me. A headwaiter simulator would also be useful. It could be wired to deliver a severe dose of humility if you couldn't read the menu and an electric shock if the tip were too low. And I'm sure we'll see others as well: maybe one for the robbers so they can decide whether or not to shoot the cop, perhaps even one for emergency room patients. I can see it now: first there'll be the roof of the ambulance, then the doctor looming over you, and then you'll get a menu of choices: "Do you want to a) Choke on your tongue, b) Go into cardiac arrest, or c) Open your eyes wide and say, 'Thanks, Doc. Say, whose pants are these anyway?' "

That Little Piggy

Never underestimate the power of the press. If at first you don't succeed, try, try again. If the trout aren't rising, fish a gold ribbed hare's ear nymph (weighted). These are lessons I learned as an investigative reporter during my time on the trail of the micro pig. The micro pig (there are actually many individual micro pigs) is a very small, very friendly variety of swine bred at the Miniature Swine Research Laboratory at Colorado State University in Fort Collins. It isn't so miniature, but, as pigs go, it's pretty small. Micro pigs weigh sixty to one hundred pounds and are bred to serve as laboratory animals for research on everything from diabetes to nutrition and exercise.

This does not, I suppose, sound like a subject for an investigative reporter. But it isn't that easy to get to see a micro pig—at least it didn't used to be. My first attempt to see the pigs (which I planned to combine with a trout fishing trip) was foiled by the forces of darkness. Someone at Colorado State had decided I might make these pigs sound too cute and that this might cause problems with the animal rights movement. My request to see the pig was refused.

I wrote a column pointing out that this sort of thing wasn't in the spirit of the Constitution (or the bylaws of Trout Unlimited, for that matter). I said a few things about the "Pork Curtain." I asked readers to mount a letter campaign. The response was . . . well, there was a response. I know for a fact that at least four people—Janice Thompson, Mrs. Kevin Martin, Tyler Suchman, and Andy Markley—struck epistolary blows on my behalf. All wrote in the spirit that Markley captured so well in his closing lines: "We want to see the micro pig! We have a *right* to see the micro pig! . . . Show us the micro pig!"

By the standards of the eighties I had clearly created a movement, if not a revolution. Shortly after the column came out, and the four letters began pouring in, Jim Bolick of the Colorado State Office of University Communications called me, apologized, and invited me out to see the pig. I knew then how Vladimir Ilyich Lenin must have felt in 1917 as he planned his trip to Moscow. Of course, the Czar never apologized to Lenin, which is why things got out of hand. It takes a big university to admit it's wrong, and CSU is a big university. In fact, Bolick not only invited me to go see the pig, but he also offered to take me fishing to make amends, since I had complained bitterly about missing out on all the giant trout I figured lived in Colorado along with those tiny pigs. After giving his offer some thought, I agreed to go see the pigs, since I felt I owed something to movement members, to the profession of journalism, and, if you want to think about it, to CSU. However, I declined the fishing offer.

I had several reasons. For one thing it occurred to me that after my first article perhaps what CSU had in mind wasn't a fishing trip but an accidental drowning. If not, well, journalists are supposed to be objective. One of the things they teach you in journalism school is that you should try not to be influenced by the benevolence of your sources into being overly fair to them. I felt I had a record to uphold. I've never been accused of fairness before, and I didn't want to start now.

So, I took the high road. No, thank you, I said to Bolick, I'll go fishing on my own. I emphasized the size and strength of my journalistic integrity (macro, very macro), and told him I would never use my position as a journalist to gain personal favors. However, I said, if by chance there were somebody at CSU in fisheries biology that I could talk to, I might like to get in a little extra work (I'm a glutton for work). Could he, I asked, set up an interview for me on the subject of current trout research. You know: Where are the big ones? What are they taking? Do journalists get to fish in the hatchery ponds? Yes, Bolick said, he thought there might be somebody available for the sort of interview I had in mind.

By this circuitous path I came, after many months, to the swine lab. And now it's my turn to apologize. In my earlier pig foray, I had had the questionable taste to wonder whether the pig was really as small as CSU claimed. That wasn't nice. Having now seen roughly 150 micro pigs I can verify that Linda Panepinto, who bred them, has indeed succeeded in developing small pigs. I find it hard to convey, for those of you who have no farm experience, what a sixty-pound adult pig looks like. The best I can do is to say that it's about the size of a beagle—an incredibly obese beagle. Since it's a pig, however, it carries the weight well. As to the whole worrisome question of cuteness in a laboratory animal, you might say these pigs are cute, but ugly cute, not cute cute. For instance, big pigs have a lot of hair. Some of these micro pigs are almost completely bald, others have scraggly wisps of hair. Remember Ho Chi Minh? Remember his beard? Well, the micro pigs that do have hair have got Ho Chi Minh's beard over their entire bodies.

The pigs also have wattles. I wouldn't mention this except for my enormous journalistic integrity, because the subject is probably embarrassing to the pigs. These aren't cute wattles. These are pendulous fleshy growths, one on each side of the head, in the general area of the jowls. Not that this makes the pigs entirely unappealing. Wattles of this sort wouldn't look good on a poodle, but on a pig they're acceptable.

I had also made some earlier noise about small pigs losing the dignity that went along with size. I no longer recall where I got the idea that pigs had dignity, but whether or not they do, these pigs do retain, by virtue of their physical characteristics, an inherent, undeniable pigness. There's something about them—some of them, anyway—that says, in a loud grunt, "I am swine."

Once I had seen the pigs the next question was as obvious to me as it would have been to any investigative reporter: Where can I catch a trout the size of a micro pig? Robert J. Behnke, professor of fisheries biology at CSU, fly fisherman, columnist for *Trout* (the magazine of Trout Unlimited), had seen me coming. In fact, I had telephoned him first. He knew I was interested in big fish. So, shortly after I sat down in his office he handed me a newspaper clipping about a trout in China that had eaten at least fifty horses and a dozen people. Normally I wouldn't believe this kind of story, particularly since it was published in one of those tabloids that usually feature items on the children of alien visitors born to earth virgins. (Who are they kidding? Virgins?) But in fly fishing (a science of sorts) it's well known that trout become fixated on the most plentiful food around (in the Chinese river, obviously horses). With smaller trout it's usually some kind of insect that's in the process of hatching—that is, going from its aquatic, larval stage to its aerial, adult stage. You try to present an artificial fly that looks like the food the trout has its mind on, and the process is called matching the hatch. This would be one hell of a trick for a fish that ate horses. But you would have to use artificials. Putting a real horse on a hook would be live-bait fishing at its most grotesque.

Behnke explained that the story was false (I knew that), although it did have a grain of truth. There are indeed big trout in China, the famed Huchin trout, which sometimes grow to a size of one hundred pounds. Not only that, but these fish also exist in parts of the Soviet Union, and, said Behnke, Trout Unlimited was in the process of organizing a delegation of American anglers to go to the Soviet Union to meet Russian anglers and do a little fishing. I assume this venture is being undertaken in the interests of international diplomacy, just as my trip to Colorado was in the interest of science and First Amendment freedoms.

Having realized that the real giant trout weren't in Colorado but in Asia, I tried not to lose heart. I went fishing, the day after I saw the pigs, in the Cache La Poudre (hide the powder) River, about an hour from Fort Collins. As to what happened that day, it all depends on what kind of a writer you are—what you put in, what you leave out, how you say it. When it comes time to talk fishing, those of us who take shelter under the First Amendment are slipperier than greased micro pigs.

For instance, I could tell you about the sun glinting off the gin-clear stream as it tumbled around rocks, and the rainbow trout flashing white under the surface as they turned in the current to snatch nymphs. I could speak of the fish rising to sip emerging midges (tiny flies—there's no end of smallness in this world) at the surface. There's a lot of this talk in fishing magazines. It's angling erotica. There was a bit of it in *Harper's* while I was on this trip. The piece was by Thomas McGuane and although it was elegant and witty, not at all the bathetic, trout-benighted ode one is apt to find in the other fishing magazines, McGuane did occasionally drift into an elegiac, almost erotic mode, lavishing on the river and its trout the kind of descriptive prose a man who didn't fish might reserve for the body of a beautiful woman.

There is, of course, another side to fishing, and women. Lust, of all sorts, often goes unrequited. Lovers get jilted, fishermen get skunked. There's bedroom slapstick, and there are the numerous accounts of fishermen who hook themselves, fall down, get wet, and drown. In this vein I could tell you about the leak in my waders, or how I fell headlong and cracked both my shins and the handle of my new fly rod. I could report the sign I saw in the first spot I fished—BIGHORN SHEEP LUNGWORM TREATMENT AREA. DO NOT APPROACH SHEEP. I could tell you how, after an hour or two of seeing, but not catching, fish I decided that fly fishing was an idiotic pastime designed for effete imitators of British royalty, and that what I really needed was a few of those lungworms for bait.

Or, if I were a good honest reporter I suppose I would stick to the facts, which are that in the end I found a better spot and I caught seven rainbow trout from eight to ten inches long using a size 14 weighted hare's ear nymph fished upstream with a strike indicator. As to how to describe the trout, they weren't macro trout certainly, but they weren't micro trout either. I've caught a lot of five-inch brookies in my day—*those* are micro trout. You could call these mini trout. Or, if you were McGuane, who described his brown trout as "short, thick, buttery"—you might call these fish, oh, I don't know, shiny maybe, or Christmas tinsel bright. Obviously, I'm not McGuane. And, although I hate to pick on the poor pig people again, I think it's cruel to saddle animals with computer terminology.

Small. That's what I'd call the trout I caught. Small.

Night of the
Living Optimists

How's this for a horror movie? A psychologist (scary already, isn't it?) develops a questionnaire to tell who is an optimist and who is a pessimist. The test is designed to benefit humanity, just like the new genetically engineered bacteria. But it gets loose and falls into the hands of the insurance industry, which uses it to develop a task force of superoptimists, men and women who will never admit defeat, who always have a cute story ready, who believe deeply in the product, whatever it is.

Cut to a shapely young woman taking a shower. The doorbell rings. She puts on a towel and goes to the screendoor. The background music is all funny chords, sevenths and ninths in minor keys. At the door is a smiling man with an unnatural resemblance (physically and philosophically) to Ronald Reagan. Crescendo. He is selling life insurance. Screams. The towel slides to the floor. He keeps on selling life insurance.

Sure, you say, it would make a scary movie, but it's like *Alien,* where the thing with the teeth pops out of the guy's chest. It's not real; it's just some writer's nightmare. It could never happen in *my* town. Well, if that's what you think, you might want to pick up Volume 50 of the *Journal of Personality and Social Psychology* and read "Explanatory

Style as a Predictor of Productivity and Quitting Among Life Insurance Sales Agents," by Martin E. P. Seligman and Peter Schulman of the University of Pennsylvania. There *is* such a test and it *has* fallen into the hands of the insurance industry.

What Seligman and Schulman did was to use the test (Attributional Style Questionnaire) on insurance sales agents for Metropolitan Life Insurance Company in Pennsylvania to find out whether they had what Seligman calls optimistic or pessimistic explanatory styles. The optimists sold more insurance and kept their jobs longer. The pessimists sold less, and presumably seeing that there was no hope of improvement for them and that it was a horrible job anyway, quit earlier. (Not that one can assume they thought they were going on to anything better.) And there is indeed a task force, although not exactly as I described it. The real one is composed of people who failed the standard industry test used to pick insurance sales agents, but whom the ASQ pegged as optimists. At last report they were doing better than anyone else.

This is only one piece of research. There are quite a few others. In fact, optimism is very big these days, because it seems that it's good for you. There's evidence that in addition to selling more insurance, optimists live longer and their immune systems work better. Not only that, but some people, Seligman among them, have suggested that one may be able to change from pessimism to optimism. I wonder. How could a die-hard pessimist muster the initial optimism necessary even to *try* to become more optimistic? Wouldn't he say: "Oh, what's the point? I'd never be able to change. I'm just a pessimist at heart"?

The optimism business seems to have begun with giving electric shocks to dogs. These experiments, which are quite famous, showed that if the shocks were inescapable the animals realized this and just gave up. This so-called learned helplessness seemed to Seligman to be somewhat similar to human depression. I guess the idea was that some humans, for whatever reasons, seemed to think of life as a series of inescapable electric shocks (I can't imagine why) and were lying down in their cages and giving up.

This perception led Seligman and others to consider, over a number of years, the ways people explain bad events that happen to them, like electric shocks. In the current formulation, an optimist, when confronted with a personal failure like not selling an insurance policy, interprets this in external, specific, unstable (temporary) terms. He says, It's not my fault; this particular customer was a jerk. The next one will be a sucker for sure. The pessimist interprets failure in internal, global, stable (permanent) terms. He says, It's my fault, I'm an idiot, I've always been an idiot, I'll always be an idiot. Oh God, there's just no point in living. Of course, there are variations, cases that are hard to categorize. For instance, somebody could come up with an internal, global, temporary explanation: I'm an idiot; there's no point in living *today*. Pessimists, since they tend to blame themselves for everything, are more likely to get depressed and give up when bad things happen to them. Optimists just whistle a happy tune and blame someone else.

What strikes me about the interest in optimism is that it is, in essence, a reemergence of the Pelagian heresy, which I thought had been taken care of once and for all at the Council of Carthage in 418. But these things never die. Other people, smarter than me (some of them anyway), have pointed out that science continually plunders the past for its paradigms. There are only so many ideas around, and they keep resurfacing with new paint jobs. In a sense, all human intellectual endeavor is nothing but one big chop shop, disassembling, repainting, and filing the serial number off old ideas—in this case the Pelagian heresy (a 1987 Nissan 300Z) and Augustinian orthodoxy (a 1936 Rolls-Royce Phantom).

I realize that not everyone has kept up with the doctrinal twists and turns of early medieval Roman Catholicism, so let me explain. The Augustinians (following St. Augustine) pessimistically believed, and still do, that each human being is born blotched with original sin and can be redeemed only by God's grace. This view is often expressed in the liturgical lament: *mea saurus, mea saurus, mea maxima saurus.** The Pelagians saw the belief in original sin as having to do with low self-esteem. (They were way ahead of their time. Of course they lived in the fifth century, when it was hard not to be ahead of your time.) They said: Hey! I'm okay, you're okay; if we just work hard and do good we can get to heaven on our own—*whether God likes us or not.* You can imagine how this infuriated the Augustinians.

Intellectual positions become transformed over time, of course, and today the issue is not salvation, but athero-sclerosis. True Pelagianism has been transformed, not so much into optimism itself, but into the medical and psy-chological belief that, if you are optimistic, you can, in worldly terms, save yourself—meta-optimism.

The original Pelagians did not fare well. They were branded heretics, which was, in those days, like having the National Science Foundation cut off your funding. Ob-viously the early bishops, and Pope Zosimus, who confirmed and validated the verdict of the Council of Carthage, felt there was some danger to the bright, happy, Pelagian ap-poach to life, or afterlife. If so, I've finally found some com-mon ground with Pope Zosimus. I don't doubt that optimism does wonders for the optimists themselves. The question I have not yet seen addressed and want the answer to is this:

*Loosely, "I'm a lizard, I'm a lizard, I'm an enormous lizard."

What does optimism do for, and to, the rest of us? Instead of thinking about the salesmen, let's think about the customers.

Who in their right mind likes a cheery, cocksure life insurance salesman? You might as well talk to a Mormon missionary. I know this seems like a gratuitous use of Mormonism, but it's not. You see, the Mormons have a history of optimism. Joseph Smith himself is an example of the most monumental optimism (or *chutzpah,* perhaps, except the word seems out of place in this context). Here was a guy who thought—in the nineteenth century—that he could start a brand-new, giant religion from scratch. And he succeeded. That's the scary part about optimists: they tend to succeed. And that means that the more of them there are out there selling life insurance, the more life insurance the rest of us are going to have to buy.

One can't fail to note that Seligman did not study shoe salesmen. Presumably this is because selling shoes isn't that stressful. One doesn't need to be an optimist to sell shoes. Why? Because people need shoes. They want shoes. They like shoes—wing tips, high tops, sandals, Hush Puppies, shoes are very popular. If you want to sell them you don't have to abuse your alumni directory and send out a bunch of form letters that start, "Dear classmate: Now that you're a father and provider it's time you began thinking about shoes." No. Shoe salesmen just sit in their stores and wait. They may wonder why their lives are spent handling other people's feet, but they're at least secure in the knowledge that as long as other people have those feet, shoe salesmen (optimists and pessimists alike) will make a living.

My feeling is that if insurance were all that great, you wouldn't have to be an optimist to sell it. Maybe insurance isn't so great, not as great as shoes anyway. And maybe optimism isn't so great either. Maybe pessimists are better for the general weal. Sure they're lousy life insurance salesmen, but so what? Balanced against this small failing is a profoundly beneficial quality that all pessimists share. They tend not to *do* much. Nowadays pretty much everything that gets done is bad, so pessimists are continually performing what you might call, to fuse once and for all the Judaic and Christian religious traditions, *mitzvahs* of omission.

For example, when there's some covert action to be undertaken, say the destabilization of the Southern Hemisphere, the bigwigs are always looking for "can do" people. What if they could only find "can't do" people? "No," the can't-do's would say, when you asked them to assassinate a foreign head of state, "that will never work. The poison will fail, the gun will jam, plus, I can't keep a secret." A pessimist president, when things went wrong, would tend to blame himself, which would be refreshing. He also might try to avoid things that could go wrong in a big way, like wars. And if we could only elect a dour, pessimist Congress, I'm sure it would refuse to fund nuclear weapons. The representatives and senators would realize, as human beings themselves, that, with the exception of those of us who are actually crooked, we're a race of fools, lunatics, and insurance salesmen, and sooner or later somebody in one category or another is going to set the bombs off.

Pessimism: it's our only hope for the future.

FOR THE BEST IN PAPERBACKS, LOOK FOR THE 🐧

In every corner of the world, on every subject under the sun, Penguin represents quality and variety—the very best in publishing today.

For complete information about books available from Penguin—including Pelicans, Puffins, Peregrines, and Penguin Classics—and how to order them, write to us at the appropriate address below. Please note that for copyright reasons the selection of books varies from country to country.

In the United Kingdom: For a complete list of books available from Penguin in the U.K., please write to *Dept E.P., Penguin Books Ltd, Harmondsworth, Middlesex, UB7 0DA.*

In the United States: For a complete list of books available from Penguin in the U.S., please write to *Dept BA, Penguin,* Box 999, Bergenfield, New Jersey 07621-0999.

In Canada: For a complete list of books available from Penguin in Canada, please write to *Penguin Books Canada Ltd, 2801 John Street, Markham, Ontario L3R 1B4.*

In Australia: For a complete list of books available from Penguin in Australia, please write to the *Marketing Department, Penguin Books Australia Ltd, P.O. Box 257, Ringwood, Victoria 3134.*

In New Zealand: For a complete list of books available from Penguin in New Zealand, please write to the *Marketing Department, Penguin Books (NZ) Ltd, Private Bag, Takapuna, Auckland 9.*

In India: For a complete list of books available from Penguin, please write to *Penguin Overseas Ltd, 706 Eros Apartments, 56 Nehru Place, New Delhi, 110019.*

In Holland: For a complete list of books available from Penguin in Holland, please write to *Penguin Books Nederland B.V., Postbus 195, NL–1380AD Weesp, Netherlands.*

In Germany: For a complete list of books available from Penguin, please write to *Penguin Books Ltd, Friedrichstrasse 10–12, D–6000 Frankfurt Main 1, Federal Republic of Germany.*

In Spain: For a complete list of books available from Penguin in Spain, please write to *Longman Penguin España, Calle San Nicolas 15, E–28013 Madrid, Spain.*

In Japan: For a complete list of books available from Penguin in Japan, please write to *Longman Penguin Japan Co Ltd, Yamaguchi Building, 2-12-9 Kanda Jimbocho, Chiyoda-Ku, Tokyo 101, Japan.*